We Girls Can Do Anything!

Being Your Best is about trying and doing. When I was about five years old, my brothers were making television commercials. But I guess I wasn't very good at it, because I didn't get any jobs. I was very little, but I decided I wanted to be in commercials, too. So I started practicing. And you know what? I got better at it. I got my first commercial!

Most of you have ideas and dreams about things you want to do. But are you afraid to try? You *can* do it! You just have to try and keep trying. Believing in yourself is the most important thing. Sure, there are girls you see at school who are prettier or smarter or who have nicer clothes. But each of us has something special to offer—because each of us is a special person. You have to figure out what is the best thing about you—and go for it.

This book is meant to help you see how special you really are.

BEING YOUR BEST:

TINA YOTHERS' GUIDE FOR GIRLS

**By Tina Yothers
and Roberta Plutzik**

AN ARCHWAY PAPERBACK
Published by POCKET BOOKS • NEW YORK

AN ARCHWAY PAPERBACK *Original*

An Archway Paperback published by
POCKET BOOKS, a division of Simon & Schuster, Inc.
1230 Avenue of the Americas, New York, N.Y. 10020

ISBN: 0-671-63128-4

First Archway Paperback printing February 1987

10 9 8 7 6 5 4 3 2

This book is dedicated to my friends and family.
Before the fame and fortune you have your friends and family.
After the fame and fortune you have your friends and family.
My most important possessions are my friends and my family.
I know that, no matter what, they will always be there for me.
This book is for Monica, Stephanie, Steve, Tina; and Mom and Dad and other Yothers.

T.Y.

For my daughter Allegra Leigh,
in the hope that she will always strive
to be the best she can possibly be.

R.P.

Acknowledgments

The authors thank the "Being Your Best" advisory board of professionals in the fields of education, psychology, health, exercise, and fashion: Jane Brodie, Ph.D., Martin Finkelman, M.D., Barbara Boychuk White, M.S.W., Ph.D., Ronni Schwartz Monsky, A.B.D., Dorothy Gurreri, M.S., Neil Baldwin, Ph.D., Marsha Hecker, and, especially, Deborah Sue Plutzik, Ph.D., of Teachers College, Columbia University, for her insightful ideas and research and for her unflagging support.

Our thanks, also, to those who believed from the start in the importance of this book: Bob and Stella Yothers, Ron Buehl, Pat MacDonald, Pat Schultz, Evan Marshall, and William Jacobson.

T.Y. and R.P.

Contents

Contents

Contents

Contents

Introduction
Being Me — Being You

I know I don't really have to introduce myself to you—but I will. I'm Tina Yothers. I am thirteen years old. I live with my parents, my older sister, and one of my older brothers in a new house on a hill, just outside of Los Angeles. On a clear day, you can see the Los Angeles skyline. I have a dog. I live in my own room, where I can hang a lot of pictures of my favorite things—musical notes and posters of my favorite rock group, Duran Duran. I like to collect pigs—stuffed pigs and pictures of pigs. I write thank you notes on pig paper. And I once had my picture taken with Miss Piggy!

Here are some other vital statistics about me:

1. I have three best friends.
2. I have to work very hard in school to get good marks.
3. I am very outgoing and I like to meet new people.
4. I have to take good care of my skin or else!
5. I like sports—not just to watch them, but to do them—when I have time.

You will learn much more about me in this book. I hope you will also learn more about yourself. You might ask, why is Tina Yothers writing this book? I asked myself the same question, because I don't ordinarily think of myself as someone with all the answers. But the more I thought about it, the more I realized that of course it should be me, because I am an average American girl who just happens to have a job and to be well known.

I wrote *Being Your Best* because girls today need someone and somewhere to turn to find out about life—what makes them happy and what makes them sad and confused. I know that reading your letters, talking to some of you on the telephone, and working with kids who have had family problems has helped me understand myself a lot better.

I get so much mail from girls who identify with me because I am not too pretty and I don't have the best shape. I think they see in me somebody they can get close to. And they are right—I have all the problems girls my age have: with my skin, weight, size, and the rest. As one girl wrote to me: "You seem to be as sincere, friendly a person in real life as on TV." Yes, I am.

Another girl wrote: "Do you think you will ever write a book?"

(How did she guess???)

I think I know about the problems younger kids face today.

I hope you will find the help *you* need in this book.

Here I am with the adorable Miss Piggy.

We Girls Can Do Anything and Don't You Forget It

Remember: This is a very special time to be a girl. Today, everybody knows that girls are just as smart as boys. We really can do anything boys can do. There are girls who play football on their school teams along with boys. There are girls who want to be scientists and doctors and airline pilots and lawyers and truck drivers and computer experts—just like boys. And they can do it if they try!

Being Your Best

Being Your Best is about trying and doing. When I was about five years old, my brothers, Randy and Cory, were making television commercials. I was very little, but I decided I wanted to be in commercials, too. I went on some auditions. Boy, was I bad! So I started practicing on my own. Then I told my dad I was ready to try again. And you know what? I got my first commercial.

Not many of you will ever make commercials. But most of you have ideas and dreams about things you want to do. Are you afraid to try? Maybe you think to yourself, "I can't do it." Or, "Kids will laugh at me." Or, "Nobody in my house has ever done this before. They don't understand."

Many of you write to ask how to get into acting. Well, for me it took a lot of time and effort since I didn't have any "connections" in the business. Basically, you get a list of agents who handle kids. You have to send them "composites," which are several photographs of you taken by a professional photographer that show how you look in various situations. If they are casting a commercial, film, or TV show and your picture fits what they're looking for, you will get called for an audition.

Many kids start out in acting by doing commercials. Michael J. Fox did, for one. And you know how big he is today! (More on Michael coming up. . . .)

My brothers really teased me when I used to practice doing commercials in the garage. But I kept on trying. I get many, many letters from girls all over the world. Some of them want to be dancers. Others want to work with computers. Or be actresses. Or writers. Or gymnasts. Or teachers. Or astronauts. But they don't have confidence. Confidence is believing in yourself. Confidence is a little voice in your head telling you, "I can do it!"

Everybody it seems has a bad self-image in some way—even me. I think my nose is too big, or that my whole body is too big. But I also try to pick out my best points and use them because you really have to like yourself to do well at anything, from schoolwork to jobs to friendship.

In show business you really have to be strong because people have a way of hurting your feelings without thinking. They forget you are just a kid.

For instance, at least once a week someone will walk up to me and say: "Michael J. Fox is just the *best* one on the show." Or, "Justine Bateman is the prettiest girl on 'Family Ties.' " I just say "Thank you." I also get these comments in letters like this one:

Dear Tina,
    I'm not exactly sure how to say this. I don't want to hurt your feelings. Well, here goes. Can you get Michael J. Fox to write to me?

Okay, if you wrote that letter to me, I forgive you, because, in fact, Michael Fox is a great person. He is humble. He does not brag about how popular he is. He is like a good teacher. I have watched and learned

Answering letters and giving my autograph are important ways to keep in touch with you.

from how he feels about being a star. He says that he is sure it is all a big mistake and one day soon he will just be an ordinary person again. The thing is, Michael still *is* an ordinary person because he is not stuck up and because he works so very hard on "Family Ties" without ever losing his sense of humor. We laugh a lot on the set together. He does not feel that because I am just a kid and he is a grown-up that he should ignore me or act stuck up. He calls me "Bear." Our dressing rooms are opposite each other. Michael has had to overcome problems of his own to be what he is today:

(Clockwise) While filming in London, the "Family Ties" family stopped for a breather; then Michael Gross and I did some sightseeing. Back home on the Paramount lot, here I am kidding around with Michael J. Fox and Justine Bateman.

he is a small person, and he was once overweight. But he never gave up his dream, which was to act.

I work with other very nice people who are like a second family to me. Justine Bateman *is* very beautiful. More important, she is very smart. She is the kind of girl who can do anything she puts her mind to. She wants to be a writer someday. She will, I am sure. Meredith Baxter-Birney works and has a big family of her own, including twin baby boys *and* teenagers. And Michael Gross, who is my best friend on the set, is just a sweet person who I can always count on. I call him "my program dad." He's my sidekick. He makes me laugh and then the director turns around and tells *me* to shush. Michael spent many years trying to make a name for himself as an actor. His determination finally paid off.

Believing in Yourself Is the Most Important Thing

Yes, you *can* do it! But you have to keep trying. We usually don't get what we want just when we want it. Sure, there are girls you see at school who might be prettier or smarter or have nicer clothes. But each of us has something special to offer—because each of us is a special person. You have to figure out what is the best thing about you—and go for it.

This book is to help you see how special you really are.

1

My Friends

W hen the song "That's What Friends Are For" was released not long ago, it made me think about what it means to have friends and to be a friend. I don't know which is more important, because we need to both give and receive. The words in the song that really got to me are:

> I'll be on your side forever more
> That's what friends are for.

It's a Big Job Being a Good Friend

Being a friend is hard work. Sometimes, try as I might, a person refuses to be my friend—and may even laugh at me for trying. Other times, a person I really don't like that much wants to be friends. I have to admit I have either ignored her until she stops trying (the way other people have ignored me) or have taken the time to find the good in that person.

I get many letters from girls all over the United States and other countries who ask me: "Will you be my friend?" Everybody needs friends, and I think that

9

even if I have never met you, by being on "Family Ties" and acting like the typical girl I am in real life, too, I am like a friend.

But that isn't quite the same thing as having a friend in your neighborhood with whom you have shared experiences and secrets.

What Is a Friend?

- A friend is someone you can have fun with.
- A friend is someone you can depend on to look out for you and protect you—and you'd do the same for her.
- A friend can make you laugh and also comfort you when you're feeling bad.
- A friend is someone you can trust.

I have two best friends, Stephanie and Monica, who live near me. I've known Stephanie since kindergarten, and it seems as if we've been friends forever. I don't remember *not* being with her. It's really special to have that kind of friend—she's almost like a member of the family.

I met Monica a few years later, in the second or third grade, when kids usually make new friends in school. The minute I talked to her I knew she was going to be a close friend. We just hit it off. We made each other laugh. We could whisper things to each other, and keep each other's secrets. When I make a good friend, I have a warm, caring feeling inside about

Here are my best friends, Monica (top) and Stephanie.

that person. It is also a wonderful feeling. It stops me from feeling lonely because I know somebody is on my side cheering for me. I also have a best new friend who is my foster sister. Her name is Tina, and I'll tell you more about her later.

Give People a Chance

Sometimes it takes longer to know if a person is a friend. There are friends of mine who are shy people who took longer to get to know. But I am a person who doesn't give up. If I meet someone who seems very nice, I am willing to be half-friends with them until they are ready to be whole friends.

Some People Will Never Be Your Friend

Then, there are people who will just never be my true friends. You might think that because I am on a TV show I have more friends than most girls. In fact, that isn't true. Often, people who are doing something special in life don't have that many friends. Other people are jealous of them or want to be their friend for the wrong reasons. If you are a girl who is very smart and gets straight A's and 100's in your schoolwork, or if you are a good athlete or dancer, you know what I mean. There will always be people who wish you weren't as smart or talented. They try to take your friends away, and they act as if you aren't very important. They act like their friends are the greatest but you're not.

A few years ago I had this kind of experience because I wanted to belong to a group that didn't want me. It was when we were rehearsing for the first season of "Family Ties" and the show wasn't on TV yet. It was my birthday. We rented a roller rink, and I invited the most popular girls in school to my party— and they didn't show up. I even had my mother drive me to their houses to get them. I guess I thought they had forgotten to come. When I got there, I could hear them laughing at me as they hid inside. Was that a bad feeling! My brother Cory felt so bad for me that he called all of his friends and I had a party with fifteen boys!

Now that "Family Ties" is a popular show, these same girls are always asking me to come over, but I won't—and I have learned my lesson about friends. Sometimes, as hard as you may try, people don't want to be your friend. You will only look silly in their eyes if you try too hard to make them like you.

Then there are the girls who worship you. Like, "Oh, Tina, you're so great!" Okay, I like myself. I think I'm pretty great, but not *that* great. I like being a person, not a princess. So I don't spend much time with people who just tell me I'm the greatest. It gets boring.

What You *Have to Give*

Each of us has special qualities that we can share with our friends. Do you know what your special qualities are? Think about it. Maybe you have a beautiful smile that makes people feel good. Or maybe you are a good teacher who helps others learn things. Or maybe you can keep a secret.

My most special quality is that I am easy to get along with. I like people and I look for good in them. I am also a good listener. I am lucky that I have always lived in the same neighborhood so I have the same friends and we are still growing together.

New Kinds of Friendship

Recently, I had a new experience with friendship. I had been volunteering at a center for kids who need help because their family situations aren't good. I felt it would be great to help one of the kids by sharing my home with her. My mom and dad agreed to let me have a foster sister.

Tina came to live with us, and I thought we would automatically be best friends, sharing everything and spending lots of time together.

It turned out we were like sisters who care very much for each other but who have different tastes. We have different sets of friends. We have different hobbies. That was hard for me to accept. I practically forced her to wear my clothes because I thought they were nicer than hers. But she felt better wearing her own things. She thought I would drop my friends and join her group of friends. But I wanted her to like my friends and all the things I liked to do.

It was hard for both of us to figure out what to do. My parents finally suggested to me that just because Tina was my roommate she didn't have to be just like me. Now we get along great: she does her stuff, and I do mine. By the time Tina went to live with another family, we found we had turned into good friends after all.

Good friends care about what happens to each other. Tina and I talk on the phone and write letters to each other, and we'll probably always do that.

Friendship Isn't Easy

What's the hardest thing about friendship besides making friends?

I think it is being able to accept the things friends sometimes do to us that hurt us. Sometimes I get angry when a friend of mine talks about me behind my back. Maybe she tells people I am stuck-up because I am on a TV show. I think to myself, "How could she do that to me? I thought she was my friend."

When that happens, you can easily make her an instant exfriend. But losing a friend is sometimes worse than forgiving her. If I am having a problem with a friend, it helps me sort it out if I write down my angry feelings in my journal. I make two lists:

1. What I really like about that person, and
2. What I really don't like about her.

I usually find that there's more good to that person than bad, and that convinces me that I want to keep her as my friend. Then I tell her so.

New Friends, Old Friends

As we get older, we will all make new girl friends in school and in the jobs we take. (Boy friends are great, too!) We will keep some of our old friends. The best way to make new friends and to keep old ones is to remember how important they are!

But how many times have you said to yourself, "I don't need that friend!" Usually you say it—I know I have—when you're in a bad mood. Maybe somebody you think is a really close friend turns down your offer for a sleepover because she's going to another girl's house. That makes you feel like you're not as important to her. Or worse, you hear that your best friend was saying some mean things about you to other kids.

You have two choices:

1. You can lose that best friend, or
2. You can find out why she is acting this way.

How do you do it? By asking her! It isn't easy to do. Most of us are too shy to ask some of the really important questions. But if it means enough to you, you have to do it. Otherwise, you will always feel that you didn't try hard enough to keep the friendship going.

My friends Stephanie and Monica are two of the most important people in my life. So when I'm a little angry at them, or a little grumpy myself, and things are not going too well between us, I will take that step—I will ask them what's wrong.

Friends Are Important

In letters that girls send me, they say that they have no friends. Some of them say they don't care if nobody likes them. That's serious! We all need friends. We all need people we can turn to. When I go to the center for abused children where I met Tina, I often meet kids who need a friend. I hope that if you are a girl with a big heart that you will think of being the friend of a girl who needs a friend.

How do you know she needs a friend? Well, you may see her on your school bus or in the lunch room or in the schoolyard and she is always alone. She might be someone with special qualities you won't know about unless you find out more about her. She might be your next best friend. So don't be shy. Tell her your name and talk to her. Let her know that you think she's okay. She may look very different from you. Her hair may be black, while yours is blond. Her skin may be a different color. Her parents may talk a foreign language at home. Maybe she even speaks with an accent you have never heard before, or prays in a way that is new to you, has different beliefs, and celebrates different holidays.

My mom tells me stories about when she was growing up in the City of Los Angeles. Her family is from Mexico. When she went to high school, she and her friend were the first Hispanic girls to go to that school. That takes courage, because there are always some people who don't want to share what they have with "outsiders." I know you are different. I know that, like me, you see that friendship is precious.

Try to imagine what it would be like if you were the new girl in your school or on your block. You would want people to give *you* a chance. So give *her* a chance. You will feel good about yourself if you make the effort. I know I always do.

Remember: It isn't always easy being a friend. But it is almost always worth trying!

Friends Who Are Boys

Boys. Do you like them? Probably just a little, sometimes more than a little! Some girls say they don't like boys. That's okay. Boys often say that about girls, too. But it's fun to have boys who are your friends. One boy who is my friend is my brother Cory. He is only a year older than me, and we do a lot of things together. He helped me get ready for the "Circus of the Stars" TV special, and he came to England with me when I was doing the "Family Ties" movie there. Oh, we fight sometimes and we get on each other's nerves.

But we like to do things together. That's what's important.

I have another special friend, a boy named Steve. He was a fan of mine at first, and when I met him we liked each other. I have gone cross-country to visit him and his family. We can talk about lots of things. For instance, he is great at sports and music, and I like sports and music, too.

But I am still very young, just the way you are. So I don't really think of myself as having a boy friend like older girls do. We have time for that when we are in high school.

The boxer Paul Gonzalez is one of my good friends who just happens to be a boy.

I do know what types of boys I like and want to spend time with, though:

1. They are kind.
2. They are generous.
3. They have good manners.
4. They work hard at anything they do.
5. They are good listeners and not stuck-up.
6. They have goals in school and in life.

Boys I Don't Like

Boys who are bullies, who try to be tough and don't care about hurting girls' feelings, are not my kind of friends. I do not care for boys who are smokers or drinkers who try to impress girls by breaking rules and laws. I hope you are never treated badly by a boy you know, because girls are special. (Boys are too.) Just remember how special you really are.

But if you are the kind of girl who is afraid even to speak to a boy, you are missing out on something fun. Think of it this way: boys are people, too. Just be yourself when you are around them, and they will appreciate you more. And you will appreciate them.

2

My Studies

To be on TV I have to keep a B average. When I got the part of Jennifer Keaton on "Family Ties," I really had to buckle down in school. I had to work much harder in school than I had been doing before to get a work permit.

I had to get my marks up pretty fast. At first, I didn't know how. These were the things I had to do:

1. I had to concentrate better.
2. I had to talk on the phone to my friends less.
3. I had to study more.
4. I had to finish my homework every night.
5. I had to do some projects for extra credit.
6. I had to try harder.

Boy, was that ever difficult! But you know what? I did it, and I felt proud. Sometimes, until we really try hard, we don't know if we can do better.

Now I have three hours of classes a day in a little office up the stairs from the "Family Ties" set. (Emmanuel Lewis used to do his work in the room across the hall!) Anyway, besides studying, I have to learn my lines and be ready to get into character whenever the director calls me to the set. Sometimes my school stuff gets interrupted right in the middle. I go to the set. I do my scenes. Then, when everybody else is ready to go home, I have to go back and finish my work.

Since the show tapes during the fall and winter, I don't get to go to regular school until March, when our "hiatus"—the show's vacation—starts. So every year it's like I am the "new girl" in school. People look at me weird. (They also probably expect that I will be stuck-up and brilliant!)

Last year, my parents considered letting me study with my tutor instead of going to regular school so I wouldn't be on display. I worried about this for seven months. But we decided I should be in regular school because a person can't run away or hide from problems. At first, I was afraid to go, because it was also my first year of junior high. The first day I had some bad experiences. One boy threw things at me and swore. Then some girl said to my face: "Oh, great, she'll be on all the pages of the yearbook." Well, I'm not even in the yearbook!

After a few days, though, everybody was just great. I even made some new friends. I became just another student trying hard to get a good report card. And you know that isn't easy!

Whatever kind of school you go to—one with a few kids or one with lots—it's still school. I remember once I asked my dad why I had to go to school, and he told me school is a kid's job, just like a grown-up's job is to have a job.

You might be like me, or you might not.

If you *are* like me, you are not the greatest student. Some days you hate school. Some days you just don't learn anything. Some days you daydream. Some days you would rather be anywhere else than sitting at your desk. But you spend about six or seven hours a day, 180 days a year, in school. That's a long time. The question is: How can we make school better? Well, let's see. First there are . . .

Teachers

What would school be like without teachers? Think about it. A bunch of kids in class. No teacher. It would be weird. It would be crazy. It would be wild. But it wouldn't be school. So let's talk about teachers.

You have to get used to them at the beginning of the year. Every year we get at least one new one. Some years we think our teacher is the absolute *best*. Some years we know we have the worst teacher in the whole school. Do you know there are ways to turn the worst teacher into the absolute best teacher you have ever had? Here's how:

Four Ways to Get on Their Good Side

1. *Give your teacher a chance*. Think what it would be like if you were a teacher. On the first day of class all these kids came in. You didn't know them.

Here I am after a mental workout with my tutor Jim Panger.

Some of them smiled at you. Some of them gave you a sneer. Some of them didn't look at you at all. You might have heard about some of the kids already and you wanted to get ready for any bad behavior. So you act tough and a little mean. No wonder the kids don't like you! In fact, my favorite teacher this year isn't popular with the other kids, who don't appreciate his sense of humor.

I can think of lots of times when I've met a person I haven't liked at first. Then, little by little, that person gets nicer. Teachers can be like that.

2. *Get to know your teacher better.* If there are lots of kids in your class, it will be hard for your teacher to get to know each one very well right away. Try to find ways to let her (or him) know who you are. Stay after school to help her/him put up a bulletin board or get the room in order for the next day. If you

do stay, make sure you ask your teacher first if it is all right for kids to stay after school, and tell her/him that you will be able to get home. Also, make sure your parents or your sitter knows where you are.

3. *Listen to your teacher—and follow directions*. Some teachers are friendly. Others aren't. Some like to talk, some don't. Some speak in quiet voices . . . some *yell*. I don't know about you, but that drives me crazy. They are tired of kids making noise and not paying attention and not doing homework. That would make anyone mad. Teachers have an important job to do. At the end of the year they have to tell their bosses just how you are doing. If you haven't learned anything they feel bad.

4. *Respect your teacher*. If you want your teacher to treat you with respect, you have to treat him or her the same way. She can't throw spitballs or paper airplanes back at you, but she can put you outside the room, send you to the principal's office, or send a report card home to your parents that says you haven't been a good kid in class. And then where will you be? Being in show business, I am more disciplined than the average girl. I know that when I am in school or on the set I don't have time to play around. There is nobody to blame but me if I don't do my job. What about you?

What to Do About an Unfair Teacher

If you think you have tried your best but your teacher hasn't noticed, if you think you are being treated unfairly, you should try to work it out first by asking to talk to your teacher privately, maybe during lunch or after school. Teachers sometimes think they know about a kid, and how well that kid is doing, but they can be wrong about you.

If talking it over with your teacher doesn't work out, then:

1. Tell your parents.
2. Ask to talk to the principal or the counselor, social worker, or psychologist in your school.

Homework and How to Do It Better

I usually have lots of it. (Besides homework, I also have to learn the week's script and blocking, so I don't have time to waste. Are you a time waster? When I was in first and second grades I didn't have much homework, but now even kids in those grades have to do more of it. Everybody wants kids to learn more, and faster.

How can you do better in school? Here are some of my ideas:

1. *Always make sure you understand the assignment before taking it home.* Don't just pretend you know what to do, because if you do that you'll end up with your workbook in front of you but no idea about how to do it.

2. *Don't depend on your parents or older brothers or sisters to do your homework for you.* First of all, they have their own responsibilities. Second of all, if

26

you let them do it, you won't learn anything. And the next night you will be behind because you didn't learn what you should have. I have a confession: once my brother helped me draw a homework assignment. I felt guilty about it. I always try to do my own work now, even if it isn't great.

3. *Make sure you set aside enough time to do homework.* It's a bad idea to come home, plop yourself in front of the TV for two hours, then eat dinner, and then do homework. By now, it's probably seven or eight o'clock. You're tired and full. Your brain is not very lively. You don't feel like doing *anything*. If you try to do homework now, you will make silly mistakes, and it will probably take you longer to finish. You'll be so far behind, you might have to miss "Family Ties"! So get a head start on homework *as soon as you get home*. Have an energy snack first, so you have some fuel to get your brain going. Do *at least* half of your homework before dinner. The rest will be a snap.

4. *Find a private place to work where people won't bother you.* I know it can be lonely to do homework, but if you are right in the middle of everybody else's chores, you'll never finish.

5. *Make sure you have paper, pencils, erasers, glue, rulers, notebooks, and anything else you will need to do your homework properly*—before the stores close!

6. *Once your homework is finished, put it in a safe place, like back your knapsack or handbag.* The "I lost it" excuse works only once.

All About Tests

Tests aren't that bad to take if you have been doing your homework and reading right along. When I am really busy with the show, I sometimes wait until the last minute to study for a quiz. Then I get nervous and try to cram all the facts into my brain at once in a very short time. *This does not work.* Sometimes I manage to remember enough to do okay on the quiz but forget everything right afterward. Sometimes, it's worse than that!

So take it from me, keep up, and then you will be able to keep on top of tests.

Tina's Ten Best Test Tips

1. Pay attention all along, not just before a test.

2. Don't be afraid to ask your teacher for extra help if you don't get something right away. Don't wait until after the test to say, "Well, I really didn't understand it. . . ."

3. Ask your teacher for a trial quiz the day before the real one to help you see what it will be like. If she can't do it, make up one yourself with the kind of questions she might ask. Do this with a friend or somebody in your family. Be tough on yourself. Don't just ask easy questions.

4. Get a good night's sleep before a test. Staying up late studying will mean you might know a little more but you will be so tired in class you won't be able to remember what that is. The best thinkers have rested brains and bodies.

5. Eat a good breakfast. It's a proven scientific fact that you can concentrate better on a full stomach. Otherwise, you'll spend more time listening to the growls than thinking about the right answers.

6. Bring enough sharp pencils, pens, and paper with you to a test. You won't be able to concentrate if you have to get up in the middle of a test to sharpen a pencil—and you will be bothering other students.

7. On a multiple choice test, even if you don't think you know the right answer, think clearly and slowly. Don't keep erasing. Stick with your first choice.

8. Have faith in yourself. If you have studied and you trust yourself, you will do okay.

9. Try not to compare grades with your friends when you get your marks on the test. If you got the best grade in the class, others will feel jealous. And if you didn't do so well, you will be the one to feel bad.

10. Everybody has good days and bad days on tests. Instead of getting down on yourself for doing poorly, promise yourself to do better next time. And ask for help *now!* That's what teachers are for.

Up Close and Very Personal: It's Called Cheating

At one time or another practically all of us have thought about how easy it would be to help ourselves along on a test by peeking at another person's paper. Some of us have probably done that already.

It's called cheating. Just as running a red light or stealing money is against the law, so is cheating. You don't get sent to jail for cheating, but you might get punished by your teacher *and* your parents.

It is also very embarrassing to be caught cheating. It is like saying, "I know I can't do this myself. The only thing I can do is get the answers from somebody else."

Tests and reports and special projects are supposed to tell the teacher how much we have learned. If we copy somebody else's work, then the teacher doesn't know what we are thinking. (And neither do we!)

Deep down, we know that cheating isn't right. It's scary, in fact. And there is another way to get the job done—by doing our work every day, as best we can. Not all of us can get all A's on our report cards. Maybe C's are the best you can do. If so, fine, as long as it is your work, and you have done it well.

After School, Alone

Lots of kids come home from school and there's nobody to greet them. If you are a "latchkey kid," you may have some days when you wish you had company. Find out if your school has any good after-school activities you can join. Or make an arrangement with a good friend to spend one or two afternoons a week at her house. There are also many things you can do to fill the time when you are alone, like reading, writing letters, making a book and illustrating it, pursuing a favorite hobby, or just plain doing your homework so when your family comes home you can spend time with them.

It is very important to make sure that if and when you are home alone you know who to call in an emergency. Keep numbers of the fire and police department, a good neighbor, your parents at work, and anybody else you might need in a pinch.

A group of kids in Texas put together the following phone tips to use when you're home alone and somebody you don't know calls up.

1. If the person tells you that he or she is a friend of your mom or dad, don't ever say that nobody else is home. Say: "He (or she) is home but can't come to the phone right now." In other words, never tell anybody you *don't* know that you are home by yourself.

2. Hang up right away if somebody on the phone uses curse words or frightens you. Then call your parents or a neighbor and ask for help.

And for you girls who have special talents, maybe your school or local community center offers after-school lessons in musical instruments, karate, cooking, acting, science, gymnastics, giving speeches, pottery making, sewing, art, and more. In the summertime, there might be camps in your area to help you learn more.

Being your best means doing the job right. As my dad says, a kid's job is going to school. Being your best when you go there means trying your hardest.

Learning Is What It's All About

In the early grades in school, everybody learns how to read and add, subtract, multiply, and divide. Then, when we get older, there are other subjects to learn. Some of them will be fun. Some of them will be hard, and maybe not so much fun.

I loved acting and I knew how good I could be, even when producers said I wouldn't make it.

Think about the things you love to learn about. Don't wait for somebody else to teach you. Use your school library to find more information.

If you are having trouble learning, tell your parents to speak with your teacher. Some kids have learning disabilities that make it hard for them to read and do other schoolwork. They are as smart as you or I, but they just can't concentrate or understand the work. Don't try to hide it if you are one of these kids, because you can be helped. It's no secret that before "Family Ties" I was an average student who didn't like school that much. I was the type of person who needed tutoring. I found out that a tutor not only can help you understand and learn but can help make the work more fun.

3

My Diet

Y ou are a preteen machine. The food you put into your mouth is the fuel that keeps you going strong.

There are lots of foods all around that are easy to eat but not very healthy. When you feed your preteen machine lots of junk food, it runs on empty.

How can you be your best if your engine is going putt-putt?

You can't.

But you can give your preteen machine a tuneup right now that will make it one mean machine.

First, you have to know what to eat.

The Foods You Need to Be Strong

There are four food groups. You should eat something from each group every day.

Group One: Fruits and Vegetables

You need four servings from this group every day. That includes all fresh stuff, frozen or canned without sugar, veggies canned or frozen without cream sauce or butter, and baked potatoes. Anything fried isn't good. My favorites: fresh carrots, celery, cucumbers, tomatoes, avocado, lettuce, green and yellow squash. Steamed broccoli, string beans, cauliflower. Baked potato or sweet potato.

Group Two: Dairy Products (Milk, Cheese, Yogurt)

You need four servings every day from this group, like low-fat or two-percent milk, cottage cheese, yogurt, frozen yogurt, cheeses. Swiss cheese is one of the healthiest cheeses.

Group Three: Breads and Cereals

You need four servings from this group, too. Look for labels that say "enriched" and "whole grain." You can find it on boxes of crackers, breads, muffins, cereals, bagels, pasta, pita bread, bagels, rice, and all the other grains on the grocery shelf, usually next to the rice.

Group Four: Meat and Fish

You need two servings every day from this group. That means choosing from fish, chicken, turkey, red meat, beans, eggs, and tofu.

Nine Not-So-Nutritious Things You Probably Eat

1. Potato and corn chips and cheese "doodles"
2. candy
3. soda pop
4. more than three eggs a week

5. hot dogs and luncheon meat
6. TV dinners
7. cookies, pies, and cakes
8. butter
9. fried foods

What about fast foods like TV dinners or burgers and fries? They are usually made with too much sodium (salt), but doctors say they are still pretty healthy. It's better to have a burger lunch than to go hungry or to eat candy bars and other sweets.

Why Is Everybody Always Talking About Going on a Diet?

I know in my family they are. My mom goes on diets a few times a year. She is on one now. She doesn't eat in restaurants right now because she doesn't want to be tempted to eat rich foods.

When you're a little kid, like under six or seven, people think it's cute if you're chubby. When I was that age, I had a little round face and body (and lots of freckles!).

"Oh, she's so adorable!" That's what I heard a lot. But now that I am older, I don't think it's so adorable to be chubby. I have grown very fast the last few years, and I am not a small person. I really have to watch what I eat. I usually eat lunch at the commissary at Paramount Studios, where "Family Ties" is filmed. If I wanted to, every day I could have burgers, fries, shakes, and other fattening food. I try not to. I try to eat a salad or a cucumber. That's my idea of dieting—knowing when to say no to too much food. Meredith is a vegetarian, and I have learned about grains, greens, and fruit from her.

Like most people, it's hard for me to stick to a good diet. Did you know that about one quarter of all Americans weigh too much and eat too much? Then there are many people who just think they are too fat. They really aren't, but they see all those pictures of beautiful, thin people on TV and in magazines. So they want to be thinner and more beautiful, too.

Tina's Facts About Dieting

1. To lose weight and look more healthy, you have to eat less and exercise more.

2. It is very, very important for kids not to be overweight.

3. If your mom and dad are on the chubby side, chances are you will be, too. But a doctor can help you figure out the right way to be the slimmest person in your family.

4. Lots of kids go through stages when they get chubby. Then, all of a sudden they have a growth spurt and lose that extra weight.

5. It is also very, very important for kids not to go on any kind of diet without talking to their doctors first.

Some girls don't do this. They just start trying to lose weight on their own. The way they do it is dangerous.

Listen to Tina:

Never starve yourself. It will hurt your body and make you weak. Being on a diet means eating good food, just not quite as much as before.

If you have a friend or a sister or a cousin who is starving herself and getting thinner and thinner, please tell somebody about it! She may be suffering from *anorexia nervosa*. Girls with that problem can't stop starving themselves.

If that friend or sister says she knows what she is doing, you should not believe her. Kids can get dizzy and feel sick and dry inside if they don't eat and drink enough. They can hurt their bodies that way and get much sicker. Don't let that happen!

Over-the-counter diet pills are dangerous for growing girls, even if they are legal. You will be depriving your body if you start depending on them.

Never eat too much and then throw up later when nobody is watching. This is another way girls think they can get thinner. It's called *bulimia* and is very dangerous. If anybody you know is trying to lose weight this way, they need help—and fast!

But if you are serious about looking your best, you might have to lose a few pounds. I know that I have to watch my weight. On the set of "Family Ties" there is a tray filled with candy and chewing gum. If I'm tired or bored, I sometimes want to eat the whole thing! But there is also a platter of vegetables. I *usually* eat them instead.

Here's what I do when I want to be thinner:

1. I tell my parents the way I feel.
2. I go to my family doctor to talk over the ways I can lose weight. He tells me how much I should eat every day to get where I want to be.
3. I do my sports activities regularly.
4. I eat more fresh fruit and vegetables as snacks and desserts.
5. I try my very best not to cheat—but I also give myself little prizes for doing my best, like a frozen fruit pop every few days.
6. I try to get other people in my family to diet with me. It's more fun that way.
7. When I get where I'm going, I end the diet.
8. After that, I try to keep eating healthy foods.

Ten Nutritious Things to Eat When You're Hungry

1. Whole wheat bread or rolls
2. Milk and yogurt
3. Chicken without the skin
4. Rice
5. Fresh fruit
6. Fresh vegetables
7. Beans
8. Water
9. Tuna fish (packed in water)
10. Pasta

Tina's Tips for Eating Better

To feel and do your best, you must eat the right foods at the right time. It's as simple as that.

1. Do I really have to eat breakfast? Yes! Not everybody likes to eat a big breakfast, but everybody needs energy in the morning. Remember that while you have been sleeping your body hasn't needed as much energy as it does when you wake up and start the day. So:

Always drink a glass of orange juice or low-fat milk—or both. If your stomach doesn't like the feel of cold drinks falling into it in the morning, have your mom heat up some milk and add a teaspoon of honey.

Always eat something that isn't too sweet, like toast or hot or cold cereal with milk.

Here are some other breakfast ideas to try:

- Plain yogurt with a drop of honey or some fresh fruit or granola mixed in
- Cheese and crackers or a grilled cheese sandwich on whole wheat bread
- Bran or corn or nut muffins
- Leftovers warmed up or cold, like cooked chicken, tuna fish, baked potato
- "Natural" peanut butter on whole wheat bread
- Grits and grapefruit
- Fresh fruit shakes you make yourself in a blender with fruit, yogurt, egg, milk, ice, and, sometimes, granola. Here's what to put in:

    1 egg
    ½ cup orange juice
    ½ cup milk or yogurt
    1 banana, cut into chunks

39

Put all these foods in a blender. If you are small, have your mom or older brother or sister help you use the blender. Be careful and cover the blender, then put it at a medium speed. Whip up the foods until everything is smooth. This is one taste-great drink, and it is also very healthy.

You can also add a spoonful of honey and a couple of handfuls of granola or cornflakes before blending. And if you want an extra-refreshing drink, add two ice cubes before you turn on the blender.

2. Don't skip lunch or stuff some cookies or candy in your mouth and call it lunch. Try for a sandwich, fruit, and milk, or a salad.

Here I am checking out California's milk supply.

3. Don't eat too many sugary or salty snacks after school. You won't be hungry when it comes time to eat a good dinner. When you buy those little packages of snacks in the deli, look on the back or have somebody else tell you whether there is a lot of salt and sugar in that snack. You'd be surprised how much of the stuff is dumped into foods we buy.

4. If you haven't eaten any vegetables or fruit all day, be sure to have some for dinner. If you don't like raw veggies, ask your mom to steam them. Broccoli, asparagus, carrots, and green beans taste great steamed. And don't forget a nice lettuce salad—without too much dressing on top!

Why Do I Have to Drink Milk?

"Kids have to drink milk." Everybody tells us that. It can get boring. Milk contains *calcium*. What does calcium do for you?

1. Calcium builds strong bones. (You need good posture!)
2. Calcium is good for your teeth. (You need a great smile!)
3. Calcium makes muscles. (And girls, we need those to be our best at sports!)

How serious is this milk thing? Very! If your mom and your grandma aren't drinking milk, get them to do it. Their bones really need the calcium in milk and other dairy products just as much as girls' bones. If you don't care for the taste of milk, yogurt, or cheese, ask your family doctor about a calcium pill that will give you your daily calcium requirement.

Dairy products that say "low-fat" on them are healthier for you.

Don't forget you can also get calcium from:

- yogurt
- cheeses, especially Swiss, Cheddar, part-skim ricotta, and cottage cheese
- oranges
- canned salmon and sardines
- broccoli, parsley, Chinese cabbage, turnip and mustard greens
- pinto beans, corn tortillas
- molasses
- almonds
- white beans, lima beans, and lentils

Quick Energy and How to Get It

I am the kind of person who is always moving, always doing something. Doing things makes me hungry. When it's not time for a meal and I need a snack, sometimes I eat junk. Who doesn't? When I can, I try to eat good snacks that don't just pick me up for a few minutes like sugary foods do, but for a long time. Even most fast food restaurants have salad bars now. A nice salad is a lot healthier than a hamburger, fries, and milk shake snack!

Try these snack foods.

- nuts (unsalted)
- raisins
- fruit
- baked potato
- peanut butter on whole wheat bread

Sometimes we dream of being somebody else. Well, you know you can't turn into somebody else. But you can turn yourself into a mean preteen machine—the healthiest possible person you can be. That means eating right.

4

My Manners

Iguess I have gotten a head start in the manners department because I have worked with adults since I was very young. They wouldn't put up with a kid who didn't act right! Most of us learn the basics about manners at home—how to eat properly, share, answer the telephone, dress, and treat guests or neighbors.

If for some reason manners aren't very important in your home, you can start to feel differently. Maybe you go to somebody's house and your table manners are terrible. Or you say things to teachers that you shouldn't. Or you have to introduce people to each other and you don't know how, so you just don't bother. Regretting it later isn't always enough. It's better to know how to act from the start.

Here are Tina's tips on good manners:

At the Table

At the table in your house, in somebody else's, or at a restaurant, sit up straight, don't wrap your feet around the chair, and don't wave around your knife and fork, or hold them in a fist. Chew with your mouth closed. Sip, don't slurp with a straw. Ask politely to have food passed to you—never reach over others to get something or use the awful word "gimme." You can never say the word "please" or "thank you" too often at somebody else's house.

Don't like the food? Don't refuse it. And don't say you hate it. Try a bite or two, and if you can't finish, quietly leave the rest on your plate. If you are visiting, don't begin eating until your host does. Place your napkin in your lap. Eat slowly.

Parties

If you are giving a party, you have a big job—to keep everything going smoothly and keep everybody happy. That means you'll have to plan the party carefully. Decide beforehand which games and records will be played and, if you're having a meal, where people will sit. If you're giving out party bags, make sure there are a few extra—just in case. When you are inviting people, make sure nobody you really like is left out. Be a good host by meeting them at the door and introducing them to your family and other friends, especially if this is a new kid in the neighborhood. Take time out from having fun to look around to make sure everybody else is, too. Help people get to know each other.

If you have been invited to a party, don't forget to let the host know you're coming so *she* can plan for you. Introduce yourself to her family if she fails to do it for you. Once there, be a good sport. Try as hard as you can to talk to other people and, if you see a shy person standing alone, to include her. Don't make a fuss if you lose a party game or think somebody else has won unfairly. And when it's time to go, be sure to thank your host for inviting you.

Sleepovers

Every family has different routines and rules. When you are invited to stay over at a friend's house, you have to keep your eyes and ears open to the way they do things. But before you get there, make sure you're prepared for the trip. It isn't polite to start borrowing the minute you arrive.

Then—

1. Unpack your possessions neatly.
2. Remember that this isn't your house. Unless invited, do not explore the house.
3. Wait to be told when to play and eat meals and snacks. Some families have rules about opening the refrigerator.
4. Wash up before meals and bedtime, but don't hog the bathroom.
5. Abide by their bedtime rules.
6. Don't be grumpy when you wake up. Say "good morning" to your friend's parents and brothers and sisters.

7. Before you leave for home, make sure you've left your room tidied up.
8. Always thank your hosts for being so nice.

The Telephone

When you are calling a friend's house, tell them who you are first, then say why you are calling: "Hello, this is Tina Yothers. May I please speak to Monica?" If you recognize the person answering the phone as a parent, be nice: "Hello, this is Tina Yothers. How are you, Mrs. White? May I please speak to Monica?"

When the phone rings in your house, answer it with more than "Hello." Never say "Yeah?" That's rude. In my house, I say: "Hello. This is Tina. May I help you?"

It may sound corny, but if the call is for your parents, they would want you to act grown-up. Then, put the phone down gently, and go get the other person. It doesn't do any good to answer the phone politely, then to scream out, "Dad!" Also, keep a pad and pencil by the phone. Take messages if you have to. Don't be shy about asking the caller to spell a name or repeat a phone number.

Talking to Each Other

Once you've said hello, it's time to say more. But what can you talk about to a new person you don't know? The best way is to ask a question or two.

47

Here are some examples:

1. Did you just move here?
2. Where did you live before?
3. What are your favorite subjects?

Or . . .

4. If you really like the person's outfit, compliment her.
5. Say something about yourself so the person can get to know you better.
6. If the person is new in school, make her feel more at home by telling her about the school and what is special about it.

If you are doing the job of introducing a parent, teacher, or other older person to a child, give the older person's name first: "Mrs. Jones, this is my friend, Ricky Smith." Then you can say, "Ricky, this is my aunt, Mrs. Jones." Remember: Always use a "Mr.," "Mrs.," "Miss," or "Ms.," when you are introducing an adult. If the adult would rather be called Walt or Sue, he or she will tell you.

It is also really important to introduce yourself when people don't know you. Don't wait for somebody else to do it. They may be too shy. Let's say you sign up late for a gymnastics class. Everybody else knows each other. So you feel like an outsider. Pick out a friendly face and tell the person: "Hi, I'm

Joanie." I'd be surprised if the other person didn't immediately tell you her name. Then, you've already got a friend.

When to Say I'm Sorry

It happens to all of us. We try to be polite, but it doesn't always work, or we forget the rules. Maybe you didn't mean to do it. You didn't know when you tattled on your little brother that he would be grounded for a week. Or you were passing notes to your friend, and the teacher made her stay after school. Or you promised your parents you'd study harder—and you didn't. Or you forgot to tell them where you were going after school and they called the police department.

Do you ignore what you've done and hope that nobody notices? Or do you figure that because you're just a kid you don't have to apologize? I hope the answer to both of these questions is no!

When I was in England making a special "Family Ties" movie, I noticed how even the littlest kids always say "Sorry" if they bump into you. You should do the same. People always feel better about what's happened if you know how to apologize.

There are some people who go around saying the word "sorry" all the time and probably don't mean it. Make sure when *you* say you're sorry that you do mean it!

Parents need to hear the word once in a while. Kids don't always appreciate how hard parents work to make kids happy and give them the things they want. Sometimes we'd rather tell them, after we've opened our birthday presents, that we don't like any of them at all. But after this outburst, you have a little ache inside. Everything is not okay. "I'm sorry" will make it better.

Saying Thanks

Nobody can read your mind. Keep some cute thank you notes and some stamps on your desk to remind you. It will mean a lot to other people if you take the time to write.

Dealing with Teasers, Bullies, and Meanies

If you are like me, you wonder why some people can't be nice. It's not just that they have very bad manners. They can't seem to get along with anybody. And they make other people's lives miserable.

If Another Kid Is Rude to You

Ignore her—or him. Sounds easy, but it is actually hard to do. That person probably wants you to pay attention to her. You would like to tell her how you feel. Instead, be strong—walk away. Let her go bother somebody else. *If you show a bully, teaser, or meanie that you are too busy to pay attention to how they're acting, they'll probably leave you alone forever.*

Should You Ever Fist-Fight with Somebody?

Some people don't think first. They get mad and jump right in with fists. They could get hurt. Besides, fighting with fists almost never makes anything better. Instead, walk away very fast. If other kids insist on fighting, ask a parent or policeman or principal to help cool them down. You would not believe how many kids give me a punch just to be able to say they hit Tina Yothers.

When *You* Become a Bully, Teaser, and Meanie

It sometimes happens. You are with your friends and somebody starts teasing somebody else. It seems like fun. You don't like to be teased, but it's different to tease another person, especially someone you know can't fight back. So stop and ask yourself, "Do I really want to do that to somebody I like?" If you can't stop yourself, at least remember to apologize later. When those rough types belt me, since I am very strong, I know I could probably clean their clocks. But fighting is ugly.

If you treat other people the way you like to be treated, with respect and kindness, you will be setting an example that everybody can follow. That's not just good manners. That's great manners. That's being your best!

5

Exercise — The Tinactivities Way

Exercise is important. Most girls know that by now. But what they don't know is that most of today's kids are not as physically fit as our moms and dads were when they were kids. Maybe it's because today we spend our time exercising our fingers in front of video games, or tuning in our VCRs and personal cassette players. Our parents drive us around so we don't ride our bikes that much anymore.

I'm lucky because I really do like to exercise, especially swimming and running. It makes me feel good just to be in motion, even when I'm just learning a new sport. When I was asked to be part of the "Circus of the Stars" TV special, I really had to shape up—and fast. I was put on a risley team. I'm sure you've never heard of risley—I hadn't either, before I started the absolutely incredibly and amazingly hard training sessions I took for three months every day after working on "Family Ties."

I needed energy and courage to perform my Risley routine on the "Circus of the Stars" show.

53

You can see in the picture of me doing the risley routine that this was no joke. I had to stand on somebody's shoulders, push off, fly through the air, flip over in midair, and then be caught by another partner's shoulders. It was scary. I wasn't at all sure I could do it. But you know something? When I finally did it, I felt great!

That's how any kind of exercise will make you feel if you do it regularly. You might think that you can wait until you are a grownup to do exercise. But this isn't very smart. Physical conditioning is important *now* because many diseases that show up later in life, like problems with your heart and weight, can be prevented by good, regular exercise. The sooner you start, the better off you will be.

Are You a Lazybones?

Some people—kids included—say they are going to exercise—starting tomorrow. Or they do it once or twice and then find excuses and stop. But your heart is really a muscle, and it needs a workout *regularly*. That is why you have to keep up the workouts for at least thirty minutes, three times a week.

Making Exercise Fun

I know that exercise can be boring, or at least not as interesting as listening to records or being with friends. So listen to records—while you're exercising.

Invite a friend to work out with you in your home, in the gym after school, or at a local health club. Start your own exercise club. My friends Stephanie and Monica help me exercise when I get lazy and put on extra pounds.

All Kinds of Sports Girls Can Do

If you don't like doing exercises, choose another physical activity that you do like—and join in. I like team sports such as softball, basketball, and ice hockey. Many community centers and schools now have regular teams for girls. Tennis is another sport that is very healthy. After a few lessons, you can really get out there on a court at your local park and start moving those muscles. And almost everybody knows how to swim. Swimming is great muscle-building exercise. When you get out of a pool, a lake, or the ocean after a good workout, you feel really strong and refreshed. If you can't swim yet, it is so important that you learn how. Lessons are not hard to find. Try your local Y.

Setting Goals

It is important when you start any kind of regular exercise that you set goals for yourself. Some of these goals should be easy to reach. They are called "short-term goals." Other goals take longer. They are called "long-term goals."

For instance, when I was doing "Circus of the Stars," my first short-term goal was to build up my muscles so that I would be strong enough to swing and climb. After a few weeks of working out with the coach, I began to feel lean and mean. My body felt so strong and powerful!

Scheduling Sports in Your Life

After doing the show, I went back to the other sports I like that are easier to fit into my schedule. You have to choose a fitness activity that fits into your schedule. Also, try to choose something that you can see yourself making real progress in. It is the everyday progress you make that will keep you going for the gold. If you have a special idol in that sport, remember that she has spent her whole life working to be the best at what she does. But you don't have to go that far to feel as if you have accomplished something special.

Count the Ways to Get Exercise

There are many ways to get exercise that you may already do with your friends, classmates, and family. Some of these are:

- Walking—a favorite of mine in the city, through the malls, and in the country.
- Hiking and backpacking
- Stationary bicycling
- Outdoor bicycling

- Roller-skating and ice-skating
- Swimming
- Jogging
- Jumping rope
- Playing tag
- Dodgeball and kickball
- Relay races
- Downhill and cross-country skiing

Can you think of an exercise activity you especially like to do and want to add to the list? Do it!

Keep a record of the time you spend working toward your exercise goals. After the first month, I am sure you will be impressed by how far you have come.

The Program According to Tina

Here's the "Tinactivities Exercise Program" that I do at least three times a week for a half-hour each time.

Tina's Important Warning: Whenever you begin an exercise program, start slowly. If you work too hard in the first few days, you will feel very sore later, and may even injure yourself. If you don't feel well, please check with your parents and your family doctor before you start doing the Tinactivities Exercise Program or any other exercises.

All exercises should begin with a slow warm-up and stretch period. This is to loosen your body and get it ready for exercise.

Remember: There is no time of day that is better to do exercises. But if you begin your day by getting your body moving, you'll find you have more pep the rest of the day. It is best to do exercises on a rubber mat or soft rug—not a concrete or wooden floor.

The Warm-ups

Start from your head and work your way down to your feet, doing each warmup for 1 to 2 minutes.

THE NECK

Roll your head in slow circles. Start by relaxing your neck and dropping your head forward and slowly continuing to roll it to the side, back, and around to the other side before it comes to the front again. Do it several times, then roll it in the opposite direction.

SHOULDERS

Lift your shoulders up and try to roll them slowly backward in a circle pattern. Then roll them forward in a circle. Then roll one shoulder at a time.

ARMS

Lift your arms straight out at your side. Try to make small circles forward, and gradually make the circles larger until they are very large. Do the same motion going backward. Remember to start with small circles and slowly build to larger ones.

WRISTS

Roll your wrists around in small circles.

TRUNK

Place your right arm behind your back and your left arm straight up over your head. Lean sideways to the right as far as possible without bending forward. Switch your arms and do the same thing to the left side.

Then place both hands over your head and bend at the waist as far as possible while you keep your legs straight. Try doing the same thing going backward but be very careful to keep your balance. Try making the same smooth circle with your trunk as you did with your head. Relax and bend forward. Let your arms stretch down close to the floor. Slowly try to make a circle with your trunk. Remember to start in front, roll to one side, to the back, and then to the other side before coming to the front again. Do this several times.

UPPER LEGS

Bend at your waist and try to touch your fingers to the floor while keeping your legs straight. If you can do this, try to put more of your hand down on the floor each time.

LOWER LEGS

Stand about three feet from a wall. Place your hands on the wall and lean forward. Remember to keep your heels on the floor. You should feel a stretchy feeling in the back of your legs.

KNEES

Bend at your knees several times, up and down, up and down. This exercise is very important.

ANKLES

Roll your ankles around in very small circles.

The Routine

Okay, now you're warmed up and ready to go. I always start off with some really easy exercises that I *know* I can do.

Sit-ups

Lie flat on the ground. While bending your knees, sit up and touch your toes. Every day do a few more, until you can do ten sit-ups.

Beginner's Push-ups

Lie face down. Place your palms on the floor under your shoulders. Bend at the knees. Support your weight on your hands and knees. Build up to 10–15 of these push-ups.

Leg Lifts

Lie on one side. Rest your head on the bottom arm, which should be stretched straight out or comfortably curled to support your head. Now lift your leg as high as you can. Try to point your toes to the ceiling. Slowly lower the leg. Build up to doing this exercise 15 times with *each* leg.

Place Running

Pretend you are jogging down the street, only don't go anywhere! Land gently on the balls of your feet. After you have warmed up, bring your knees up higher and higher. Keep it up as long as you can.

After you have gone through these exercises, try my zoo routines. They're fun and they're healthy. They are also a great activity to do with your best girl friend after school or on a sleepover. Get out your camera and take silly pictures of each other. But always remember to do the Tinactivity warmups first and to do all exercises on a soft rubber mat, mattress on the floor, or soft rug.

The Crabwalk

Squat down, then reach back. Put both hands on floor.
Don't sit down! Walk like a crab, backward, forward,
to the sides. Keep your body straight.

Seal Crawl

You already know how to do a beginner's pushup. So do it, then keep your body straight and walk forward on your hands while dragging your feet. Keep your head up.

Being Your Best

Mule Kick

Hee-haw. Stoop down, with your hands on the floor in front of your feet. Support your body with your hands and kick out with your "hind" legs.

Pretty Pony Rock

Stretch out your whole body and arms. Arch your back and rock back and forth. Let somebody give you a little push to get you going if you need it.

The Swan

Lie face down. Stretch your arms out to your sides, palms down. While keeping your toes on the floor, raise your head, upper back, and arms up so you look like a beautiful swan. Count to two, then relax your body. Do this exercise 8 times.

Being Your Best

Whenever you have finished any exercise routine, it is important to do some cooling-down exercises. Use the warm-ups we did. You must prevent cramps by putting on a jacket and some jogging pants while you cool down. When you want to feel relaxed, try this very quiet exercise I learned when we had an exercise class at lunchtime on the "Family Ties" set.

It is named after a beautiful flower and is called the Half Lotus. It is so simple and so relaxing. Afterward, you'll be ready for a hot bath or shower.

Half Lotus

Sit with legs crossed. Keeping your back straight, close your eyes. Place your wrists on your knees. Make a tiny loop with each thumb and first finger. Just sit like this for about 60 seconds. Relax.

One other great exercise activity I want to talk about is something girls have been doing for a long time. It's a great sport if you live in a city because you can do it on an asphalt sidewalk. You can do it just as well on grass or earth. And on wood floors, too.

You will find that the more you do it, the faster and stronger you will become. I have a good friend, Paul Gonzalez, who won an Olympic medal in boxing at the 1984 games. I sometimes work out with him by doing this exercise. It also improves posture. It doesn't cost anything, because you can use any old piece of rope or clothesline. When you step on the middle of the rope, it should come up on each side to your armpits. If the rope is too long, wrap the ends around your hands. All you need now are sneakers to protect your feet or a thick, rubbery mat. What is this sport? It's called Jumping Rope.

Jumping rope is a good warm-up activity if you like to jog. It is also a good activity *after* you've done the Tinactivities warm-ups, as your main form of exercise. (When you're finished, remember to do some cool-down exercises.)

There are two basic steps you have to learn:

1. *Skipping Rope.* Put one foot in front of the other as though you are going to skip. Start looping the rope around you as you do this.

2. *Jumping Rope with Feet Together.* Keep looping the rope while your feet are touching each other.

After you learn the basics, try some of the many great jump-rope stunts like the Criss-Cross, Toe-to-

Toe, Double Jumping, and Double Dutch. Many schools and community centers have jump-rope teams. Not only will you have fun with other girls, but you will be getting very healthy.

Jumping rope is one of the most complete exercise activities a girl can do.

6

My Clothes Closet

Now that you're getting in shape and eating right, it's time to concentrate on clothes—how to buy them, how to wear them.

I'll tell you a secret: I love clothes! When I'm dressed in an outfit I like, I feel great. And of course I look great! You will, too.

One reason this is a really exciting time for girls is because there are so many great clothes to choose from. Here's what I think:

1. Knowing about fashion is part of being a smart person.
2. Knowing what looks good on *you* is an important part of being fashion-smart. I mean, it's great to compliment your friends when they dress great, but it's more important to figure out how you can be one terrific-looking girl.

Choosing Clothes That Look Great

Wow. That's a tall order, I know. Especially because everywhere we look, people are telling us what we *should* wear and what we *should* buy. If you look in magazines, you see all kinds of clothes. The advertisements tell you to buy this, to buy that—buy it all! I'm sure you know the feeling. You're watching TV and these commercials come on for some great running shoes. At that moment, you think you'll die if you don't get a pair.

Or you're flipping through a magazine and you see this great shirt on a girl just your age. For example, you think to yourself, "I love that big shirt the model is wearing! I'm going to get one just like it."

So you go out and buy that big shirt. You're so excited about it that you don't really stop to look at yourself carefully in the mirror and ask:

"Does this shirt look good on me?"

Don't get mad if I say this—but maybe not!

If what you're getting makes you look too big or too small, too chubby or too scrawny, then it isn't a style right for you. If you buy it, you *will* succeed in being trendy. But you may not look as well as you could in the right clothes for you.

Sometimes it takes somebody else to tell you that you have made a mistake. But listen when they do (instead of getting mad at them). Then make your own decision about how you want to look.

For instance, I am a tall girl for my age. I think I

have big shoulders and that my arms are a little too chubby. So I don't think I look right in tight sweaters and blouses. So I say, okay, I'm tall, my shoulders are big. I'm not perfect. I also know that I have long legs and that my waist and hips are okay, so pants look good on me.

I am also fair-skinned and my hair is light, too. Some colors make me look too pale. I like my clothes bright and happy. When they are, I actually feel brighter and happier. I can get up on a cold day, put on a bright sweater, and I can feel my spirits rising.

On "Family Ties" I don't wear the same types of clothes I wear in real life. I like jeans and running shoes. I like loose sweaters and sweatshirts and soft, silky overshirts with designs and pretty prints on them. I love jeans and tapered pants. I like cottony summer clothes. Since I am a girl who likes to *do* things, I like it if my clothes can "run with me."

Getting to Know Clothes

Here are some of my favorite ways to learn more about clothes:

1. I like it when my mom or my older sister go shopping with me because they sometimes have good ideas. We all have fun together when we share our ideas. Of course, I have ideas, too, about what looks right on me. So I think about what they say—and sometimes I listen to it.

2. I like to window-shop. You can discover a lot

just by looking—like what the "in" colors are, and how they are being worn.

3. I like to watch people on the street, in the movies, on TV. Wherever you go, you can find ideas.

4. I like to look through fashion magazines, especially *Seventeen, Young Miss, Teen, Elle,* and, when I was younger, *Barbie,* and any other ones mom may have. Keep a scrapbook of the great things you see. Or get a big piece of brown wrapping paper and paste up on your wall your favorite pictures of clothes from magazines.

The Great Clothes Quiz

Now that you know what's happening in fashion, you have to buy clothes that don't just look good on models in pictures. They have to look great on you, too. Get out a pencil and paper and use this space to write in when you answer these questions before you go shopping:

1. What kinds of clothes do you like?

2. What are your favorite clothes?

3. What are the names of the fabrics you like best? (If you don't know the exact names, describe how the fabrics feel and look.)

4. Are they easy to wash and dry and keep ironed?

Shopping Smarts

Now you are ready to go shopping. When you are in a store, ask yourself these questions:

1. Do I really really like it? Or do I just *think* I should like it, because I saw it in a picture, or a friend just got it, or my mother wants to buy it for me?

2. When will I wear it? I like to own a few things to wear on special occasions. But most of my clothes are for everyday.

3. How does it look on me? Sometimes I try something on and I really want to buy it because everybody else has it but it doesn't look too good on me. If that little voice is saying, "Tina, this isn't really great," should I pay attention to it? Yes!

4. Is it well made or junky? How much something costs doesn't always have much to do with how it is made. You can find some great clothes in discount

department stores if you choose carefully. Expensive clothes don't always look better.

Look Bright! or, All About Color

Color makes a difference. Color is fun. Colorful clothes make you stand out.

Here are some of my favorite color combinations. See if you can mix and match the clothes you already have to come up with some pretty combinations. Do the same when you buy new clothes.

1. yellow and black
2. purple and pink
3. red, royal blue, and yellow
4. black and white

What are some of your favorite color combinations? Write them down here:

When you are going shopping, look in your closet and drawers and see what you already own that you can match up to something colorful. Take that shirt or skirt or pants or vest with you to the store.

Plaids, Stripes, Flowers, and Blobs — "Mix and Match" Rules

Rule #1

If you are wearing a blouse with a plaid, striped, flower, or colorful blob design, your pants or skirt should be one solid color. That color should match one of the colors in the plaid, stripes, flowers, or blobs.

Mix and match: bright top, solid bottoms.

Rule #2

If you are wearing pants or a skirt with a plaid, striped, flower, or colorful blob design, your top should be one solid color. The top should match one of the colors in the plaid, stripes, flowers, or blobs.

Rule #3

You can break these rules if what you are wearing absolutely matches because it is a set. Then the plaids, stripes, flowers, or blobs will look great.

Rule #4

You can have tons of fun matching up things. For fun, open your closet and drawers and try to make some new matches you never thought of before. I bet you will discover some really great combinations.

Girls and Pink

Girls, pink is "in" (again). Think pink. It looks great with most other colors. It looks great on most girls, whether you have light skin or dark skin. I am happy to say that pink is great for girls. Let's wear it with pride! It's my all-time favorite color!

Girls and Black

Not so long ago, girls never wore black clothes. Parents thought that this color was too dark and sad for kids. But not anymore. Black is a beautiful color. If your mom doesn't like you to wear black pants or shirts or sweaters, try some black accessories. They really make outfits look super.

Accessories, or, What To Wear with Your Clothes

Accessories are everything you wear besides clothes. Accessories are: socks, necklaces, bracelets, pins, rings, scarves, stockings, leg warmers, gloves, hats, barrettes, purses, knapsacks, headbands—you name it.

Accessories are fun, and they are also very important. For instance, let's say you have an old outfit that is very boring—like a plain blouse and a pleated skirt. You can make it fun again. Here's how:

1. Find a nice, bright scarf to tie around your neck.
2. Add some colorful socks with a great design or little fake jewels on them or some great tights with hearts or bows on them.
3. Try on a pretty belt.
4. Match a string of beads to the color of the belt.

Places to Look for Accessories You Can Buy with Your Allowance

Kids didn't wear very many accessories before. But now they do and so:

If you go into any store you will see lots of

Accessories, like my necklace, really complete an outfit—and they can be great conversation pieces.

accessories made *just for girls*. Some of them can be really expensive, though. Very often, in a basket right next to the cash register, or on a table in the back of the store or girls' department, there will be stuff on sale. Don't be afraid to look through it. You'll be surprised at what you'll find.

Sometimes, you will even find wool scarves, ski hats, mittens, gloves, belts, headbands, umbrellas, sunglasses and regular glasses, socks (and yes, even clothes) in the boys' department.

My favorite places to find accessories are at rummage sales. Look for signs people paste up on street corners. Sometimes they put little ads in the newspaper about them. These sales are held in your local town hall or church or synagogue. Garage sales are good, too. For very little money, you can buy beautiful old necklaces, rings and pins, scarves and belts, purses and bracelets.

Don't be too shy to "bargain" with the person who is selling the stuff. She or he probably just wants to get rid of it. If you only have fifty cents or a dollar, tell her so. She will probably sell you that great necklace marked for two dollars for much less.

And don't forget to ask mom, grandma, or anybody else older to let you know if she wants to get rid of any of her accessories. You just might find what you're looking for, like that red bandanna she never wears, or the shiny patent leather belt she got tired of. You can cut it down to your size.

Remember #1: Accessories give you a "total

look." They can make you stand out in a crowd. And they are so much fun to wear.

Remember #2: Keep your accessories in a special place. That's because some of them are so small you can lose them.

"Looking Great" Checklist

Most girls don't have that much money to buy things. But you don't need that much to look good. Here is a list of the important clothes you need to be your best. Since your mom or another adult will probably be helping to buy the stuff you need, show them this list and talk over what you will need during the school year. You probably own some of these things already, so make a checklist.

	Have It	Don't Have It
1. One basic inside jacket (a blazer)	☐	☐
2. Two skirts (solid colors)	☐	☐
3. One pair of nice pants	☐	☐
4. Two pairs of jeans (one denim, one corduroy)	☐	☐
5. Four tops: One dressy, one sporty, two for school	☐	☐
6. Two sweaters	☐	☐
7. One pair of running shoes	☐	☐
8. One pair of "school shoes," like slip-ons, straps, or ties	☐	☐

	Don't
Have It	Have It

9. One pair of party shoes (black patent leather shoes never go out of style) ☐ ☐

10. One jogging outfit (pants and sweatshirt) ☐ ☐

11. Outside jackets: one for cold weather, one for warm weather ☐ ☐

12. One special party outfit ☐ ☐

13. One pretty nightgown and robe for overnights with friends ☐ ☐

14. One rain slicker ☐ ☐

15. Accessories you can use with all of the above ☐ ☐

With these clothes and accessories you can create many different "great looks."

In the summer, add these clothes:

	Don't
Have It	Have It

1. Three pairs of shorts ☐ ☐

2. Three t-shirts (different colors, of course) ☐ ☐

3. Three cool tops (halters or sleeveless) ☐ ☐

4. One bathing suit ☐ ☐

5. One super beach towel ☐ ☐

6. One pair of sandals ☐ ☐

	Have It	Don't Have It
7. One sundress	☐	☐
8. One pair of canvas sneakers	☐	☐
9. One pair of sunglasses	☐	☐

But I'm Too Fat to Wear Nice Clothes

Sometimes I feel that way. Many girls do. They write to me and say they are overweight and they don't know what to do about it. Sometimes their parents don't want them to change. Sometimes the girls, themselves, are scared to lose weight.

It is hard to be a growing girl and to feel that you do not look as good as other kids because you are chubby. Remember, when it comes to clothes, if you are chubby and you wedge yourself into clothes that are too small they will make you look bigger. So be comfortable in what you wear.

But if you are not ready to have your doctor put you on a healthy diet, and you are not ready to try to cut down on how many sweets you eat, buy your clothes in stores where there is somebody nice to help you. That person will find you clothes that *fit*. She can be your shopping friend, somebody who will help you look your very best even if you don't really feel your best. Later on, when you and your parents are ready, you will be ready to change, to eat less, and to look the way you want to look.

There are also some girls who like being heavy.

That is fine, too. The world is made up of all kinds of people. Not everybody can—or should—look like a fashion model!

Fashion and Neatness

You can have the prettiest clothes, but if you don't keep them clean and washed and ironed—and you don't keep yourself smelling and looking fresh—then you've got trouble. Take pride in the things you have. It's easier to drop your clothes on the floor when you come home from school. But the next time you want to wear them, they just won't look as good. Keep your body fresh and clean. Wash in all the right places.

Your Parents and Your Clothes

Sometimes there's trouble. Your mom or dad won't like what you want to buy or what you're dressed up in. Usually they complain that kids always want to buy fads. Fads are what everybody likes. That's why we want to wear them. It makes us feel like we are part of the group. It makes us feel like we belong. So remind your parents that kids like to dress like each other. It's the parents that don't.

Also, when you borrow your mom's clothes, treat them with respect!

Remember: When you are dressing, take chances. Have fun with your clothes and accessories. Be bright! Be your best!

7

Parents, Brothers, Sisters

When I began working with kids who don't live with their parents because of family problems, I realized that many children don't live in a house with a mom, dad, sisters and brothers, or a grandparent.

Today, there are many different kinds of families. That means the word "parents" has changed.

1. Sometimes it means having two of them in the same house.

2. Sometimes it means having only one parent living with you. Your dad or mom may live in another house or apartment in the same neighborhood, across town, or in a different city.

3. There are also kids whose parents can't care for them properly, so the kids must live in foster homes with people who are temporary parents, or group homes with "house mothers" and "house dads," who are sort of like counselors at camp.

4. Other kids are adopted, so they have natural parents they may not know or never have met and adoptive parents who raise them.

5. Kids whose parents are divorced sometimes have a stepparent or even two if their father and mother both have married again.

6. Other kids find a relative or family friend they can get close to. That person can be like a parent in many ways.

When my mom and dad were in school, most kids lived with their natural parents. There were not very many kids who had only one parent or no parents. If you were one of these kids, you probably felt really alone. But now that so many kids have so many different kinds of parents, it's not so strange. In fact, the newspapers say that by 1990, in some big cities, there will be more kids living with only one of their parents than there will be living with two!

I feel I am very lucky to have two parents in my house. I love them very much, and I know they love my three brothers and sister and me the same way, and I hope they will always love each other.

But let's face it, parents are people, too. I think that is what most kids never think about, including me—unless my mom or dad remind me, usually in a loud voice.

Since parents are people, their personalities aren't all the same. Some of the girls who write to me talk about their parents.

"My parents ignore me twenty-four hours a day," one girl said.

"My parents won't let me do anything alone or just with my friends," another told me.

"My mom tells me what to do all the time," a third girl wrote.

"My dad is never satisfied with my schoolwork," said another.

"All they do is yell at me," wrote a fifth girl.

Pick Out Your *Parents — and Figure Out What to Do About Them*

Your letters made me think about the different kinds of parents there are in the world. Though all of us would like to live with perfect parents, they are usually like the people I will describe below:

Preoccupied Parents

They are so busy and wrapped up in keeping the house running and the family fed and their jobs going that they tend to ignore the kids. Even if they don't say to you, "Don't bother us," you usually try to work it out yourself. But you don't know everything. You're just a kid. You make mistakes and you feel like you need more help and love.

WHAT TO DO ABOUT "PREOCCUPIED PARENTS"

Tell them how you feel—that you know how busy they are and how much they have on their minds. Tell them you need some time alone with one or both of them. If they depend on calendars to keep track of everything they do, ask if you can be one of their regular appointments. Maybe you can go along on some grown-up errands, just to be with them for a while. If they say they can't fit you in at all, who else do you know who *can* "fill in"—a grandparent, older brother or sister, cousin, aunt or uncle, neighbor or teacher?

Expect-a-Lot Parents

You feel that whatever you do, it isn't good enough to please them. If you study hard and score a ninety percent on a spelling test, they wonder what happened to the other ten percent. Maybe they compare you to somebody else in your family with special talents. Parents of this kind want you to be so good at everything you do, but they make you too scared to do your best. They may even punish you if you don't.

WHAT TO DO ABOUT EXPECT-A-LOT PARENTS

Most parents want their kids to be better and stronger and smarter than they are. They feel proud if we do our best. They feel let down if we don't. Sometimes they think we're not trying hard enough. That may be true. But sometimes, as hard as we do try, we still don't please them. If you have an expect-a-lot parent, you need to sit down for a talk. Ask them why it is so important to them that you do better. Tell them how hard it is for you to do your best if they never think it is good enough.

Nagging Parents

There's at least a little bit of nag in every parent, especially if you are a kid who doesn't listen all the time, doesn't make your bed, or do your homework or do other jobs kids tend to have to do. The real nagging parent never lets you forget just how many things you have yet to do. You can get to feel that nothing you do is quite right. You eat too much, too fast, without any manners, with dirty hands, and you chew with your mouth open—for instance. Parents like this feel it is really important to do *everything* right so when you are grown up, you will have all the right manners and ways of doing things. But right now, you just don't feel like it. So you tune out. And the nagging goes on.

WHAT TO DO ABOUT NAGGING PARENTS

Parents like this are often called "per-fec-tion-ists." If you don't do things the right way, they just get more irritated. When they get more irritated, they nag harder. Tuning out only makes it worse. Think about what they are saying. Would it be so difficult to chew with your mouth closed, or wash your hands before dinner, or eat a piece of fruit for a snack instead of a cream-filled donut? Probably not. What about at least smoothing your covers, even if you can't make your bed perfectly? That's an improvement over a rumpled clump of sheets and quilts. Hang up your skirt after school? Put soiled clothes in the hamper? Start your homework without being told?

Follow-the-Rules Parents

They have a rule for everything, and if you don't follow it—watch out. No TV on weeknights. No staying up late. No friends for sleepovers. No sweets. No fun. Follow-the-rules parents love to ground kids.

WHAT TO DO ABOUT FOLLOW-THE-RULES PARENTS

First, you've got to ask yourself, "Why are my parents like this?" It could be that they are worried that something could happen to you unless they act strict. Or maybe their parents made them follow rules. Whatever the reason, "follow-the-rules parents" are tough to deal with. Maybe they don't realize how tough it is for you. Tell them how you feel. Talking about your feelings is always the first step to working out a problem.

Give-You-Everything Parents

Now that you think about it, there's nothing your parents wouldn't do for you. They write notes to the teacher asking her to excuse you if you don't finish your homework. They buy anything you ask for. Clothes. Toys. *Everything.* You've got the biggest allowance on the block. Living with people like this is actually kind of boring. You wonder what it would be like to work hard for something. Then your parents get angry when you don't just love everything they buy for you. The question is, do you have a right to complain? Or are you just being a spoiled brat?

WHAT TO DO ABOUT GIVE-YOU-EVERYTHING PARENTS

This is a hard one. Some give-you-everything parents do it because they are trying to make up for not having anything when they were kids. Others just want you to have the best. Still others think that since they don't have time to spend with you, giving you everything makes up for it. Well, give-you-everything parents need to sit down with you for a conference. I bet they will be surprised when you tell them you don't want everything, even if you ask for it! Tell them you appreciate all they do for you. Tell them you want to find out how it feels to work. Can they give you some jobs around the house? Can they save some of those big presents for holidays? They probably will be relieved.

Scaredy-Cat Parents

They are afraid to let you do anything. Your friends get to go places and do things, but you don't. You can't go on overnights or on class trips. You can't ride your bike around the neighborhood. There are lots of things you can't do because your parents are afraid of what might happen.

WHAT TO DO ABOUT SCAREDY-CAT PARENTS

First, you have to prove to them just how capable you are. Ask your mom and dad to come with you around the block. Prove to them that you know your way around. Take the responsibilities you are given very seriously. Once they see how much you care, they will start letting up. It may take a while—so don't give up.

Different Parents

Different parents aren't like anybody else's parents. They have a foreign accent. They work nights. They have an old, beat-up car. They are just different, and you wish they were the same as everybody else's parents. Why did it have to be you who got the weird ones? Tell them you love them very much, but you feel embarrassed about how they talk or act to your friends and teachers.

WHAT TO DO ABOUT DIFFERENT PARENTS

You may think that you're the only one with parents who aren't like anybody else's. But almost every other kid would probably tell you her parents are different in some ways, too. Besides, being different is interesting. Being the same as everybody else is boring. I am glad my parents are just a little different— that my mom is Mexican and my dad comes from the Middlewest. When I was a little girl and my dad was traveling as a musician and wasn't always home, I wished he was with us. But when he came home with stories about traveling and meeting people, it was worth it. So, you see, being different from the neighbors means being special. Help your kind of "different" parents to learn more about your life.

The Greatest Parents in the World

I bet you wish you had them, even just one. There are times when we do think our parents are great, but in between it always looks like somebody else got those great parents.

Well, I wonder if there is such a thing as the world's greatest parents.

There are some parents who can buy their kids anything. Are they the greatest? Maybe they are so busy making money and working that they don't have time to spend with their kids.

There are some parents who don't have much money at all. But they eat dinner every night with their kids and have time for them on weekends. Maybe they are the world's greatest parents.

What I really think is that each of our parents is a little bit great. If we show them our love and try to be good kids, it will help them through the rough times and make the great times even better.

You will not always agree with what your parents tell you. But now is the time to listen to what they say. Soon enough you will be a teenager. If you think being seven or ten or twelve is hard, wait until you are a "teen."

If you realize that your parents are your friends and not against you, you will be way ahead when you are a teen. Teens have to make lots of choices. The better you learn how to make choices now, the easier it will be for you when you are a teenager. I know, because for me it's happening right now!

Brothers and Sisters

I come from a big family. Sometimes it's lots of fun. Sometimes it isn't. If you want to be alone, brothers and sisters are usually in the way. When you want company and your brothers and sisters aren't there, you can feel suddenly very lonely.

When brothers and sisters get along with each other, the feelings you feel are warm and loving. You can do things together, like when my brother Cory helped me practice for the "Circus of the Stars" competition.

We Forget How Much We Love Them

But because brothers and sisters are always around, sometimes it's easy to forget how much you care about them. Instead you fight over little things—what's yours, what's theirs. By the end of the argument, you can't always remember why you were so mad. (My biggest fights with my sister are about sharing our clothes.)

Maybe there are other reasons, too. Like:

1. You think they are getting more attention from your parents than you are.
2. Their report cards are better.
3. You think they are handsomer or prettier or that they look better in clothes.
4. Maybe they ignore you.
5. You share a room and you want a place of your own.

My brother Cory (who has gotten much taller since this photo was taken) is one of my best friends.

There are tons of reasons for not getting along with brothers and sisters. But there are also tons of reasons why you should try harder so that you do get along. Besides, brothers and sisters are important, and they will be important to you your whole lives.

Hey! Can't You See I'm Growing Up?

Those of you who, like me, were born last in the family, know that it isn't easy being a "little sister." At first, when you are really little (like five years old), it's nice when everybody treats you in a special way. Maybe you get taken out for ice cream, or your big brothers and sisters buy you things and bounce you around on their laps. But when you get to be ten, eleven, and twelve and you feel grown up in so many ways, it can be strange to have people treat you like the "baby."

But I remind myself that they do not mean to hurt my feelings. There are ways I can remind them that I am grown up—without hurting their feelings.

What I really want is to be treated as an equal. When I want to be heard in a big family where often several people (older than me) are talking at once, I ask dad or mom if we can have a *family meeting*. Try one at your house, once a week or once every few weeks. Sit around the table or in the living room. Each person gets to say what's bugging her (him), and what's going on in her (his) life. You will be amazed at how much you can learn about the family, and what they will learn about you. Later, you will probably hear them whisper, "She really *is* a big girl now!"

"She's Some Sister": Six Ways to Impress Your Family

1. *When brothers or sisters make you angry, count to ten* (to yourself) before getting angry back at them. You probably won't get as mad as you thought you would.

2. *Give a brother or sister time to be alone*. Everybody needs quiet time and privacy. It doesn't mean they don't love you if they go off by themselves.

There are times when you will want to be alone and you will want them to cooperate.

3. *Don't borrow their property without asking.* You wouldn't want someone to borrow your favorite outfit, video game, book, or anything else precious to you, without checking first. Respect their possessions—and they will respect yours.

4. *Be a good listener.* Brothers and sisters sometimes need someone to talk to. You can be that special person. If your brother or sister is younger than you, you will probably be able to guide him/her to a better decision because you have more information about things. If she or he is older, then they probably want you to be understanding. If you ever have advice that will be helpful to them, or can protect them, give it.

5. *Be able to take a joke.* If you are the youngest, you may be the person your brothers and sisters make fun of, but they probably don't mean to hurt your feelings. Try not to let every little thing upset you. If you're older, be careful about making jokes at other family members' expense. Be careful and be kind. In my family you have to be able to take a joke because we're always playing them on somebody. When my foster sister Tina came, she had to learn this—the hard way!

6. *Do something really special for a sister or brother once in a while.* Compliment them. Tell them how important they are to you. Help them clean their room. Lend them money. Give them homework tips. Or make them a snack. Here are two great ones that are bound to surprise them:

The Let's-Be-Friends-Again Shake. It's a purple milkshake, as healthy to drink as it is wild to look at. You need:

3 tablespoons frozen grape or orange juice concentrate

2 cups vanilla ice cream

1 cup milk

Put these ingredients in a blender and whip until creamy smooth. Serve immediately. You will have two portions—have a drink together!

Peanut Butter Pizza. That's right! Buy a prepared pizza crust, usually found in the frozen food department of your food store. Or make your own from scratch (if you promise to clean up afterward!).

- Spread a mixture of peanut butter and honey on the crust.
- Sprinkle coconut flakes, raisins, nuts, and fruit chunks on top.
- Spread some shredded mozzarella cheese over the top.
- Bake about 8–10 minutes.
- Eat it together!

Some Parents Don't Live in the Same House

My parents have been married a long time and they are still married. But today there are many, many children whose dads and moms do not stay married. No matter how many kids you may know who have parents living in different houses or cities, if and when this happens in your own family, it is really scary.

I know this because when I was seven I acted in a movie called *Shoot the Moon*. I played a little girl whose parents get divorced. The dad goes to live in an apartment with his girl friend. The mom stays with the kids. The dad picks the kids up for school in the morning and takes them on weekends. Each of the kids feels sad and strange about what happens. They still love their dad very much. They know he loves them. But they are living with their mom. She isn't very happy, and they want to protect her and help her. They also don't know how to act to their dad's new girl friend. She is divorced and has a little boy. You can see it is a very complicated situation in the movie—as divorce is in real life.

Kids often don't understand what's happening when parents split up. They blame themselves. They figure if a parent can leave another parent, it is only time before the parent will also leave the kids. They often feel they have to decide which parent to love more. Some kids try to get the parents back together again. Others just won't admit what is happening is true. They don't have anybody to talk to about how they feel. Sometimes, the kids are the last to know that their parents are not going to live together anymore. Sometimes, they know something is very wrong, but nobody will tell them what it is. Very often, the parents are too busy worrying about themselves, feeling guilty about what is happening, and too busy deciding what to do next to pay attention to the kids.

Sometimes, it's really better for the family if parents don't stay married. If parents fight and hurt each other or hurt the children, everybody actually feels relieved when all that stops. But no matter how sad a kid can feel if her parents can't get along, it usually seems worse for you when one of them leaves—because you still love them both very much.

Here are some good things to remember if your parents can't get along and decide to live apart.

1. It is all right to feel upset, afraid, confused, and alone. Your parents and brothers and sisters probably feel the same way, even if they don't say so. It will also make you feel better to cry.

2. It is all right to still love both your parents—even if one of them has hurt the other one, and you.

3. It's also all right to be mad at one parent—or both of them. But it is also all right to forgive them.

4. It is natural to feel responsible for your parents' problems—but you aren't to blame.

5. It is natural to want to talk to the parent who has moved away and to want to know that he or she is okay. Make a phone call.

6. If your parents fight all the time and are sometimes violent with each other or with you and your brothers and sisters, it is natural to feel scared. Of course your parents love you, but they may be so angry with each other and with what has happened to them that they can't control their emotions. Please tell somebody you trust what is happening so that you can be helped before you are hurt.

7. It is natural to feel ashamed that your family is breaking up. Some kids you know may not be allowed

to play with you anymore because their parents think divorce is catching. Not only is that not true, but it is hard to take. Remember there are many other kids who are just like you. Find out who they are.

One of the most important things you can do at this point is to talk to somebody about how *you* feel. If it's too hard to talk to your parents, don't be shy to ask a grandparent, a neighbor, an older brother or sister, a good friend, or a teacher you trust.

When you open up, you will soon find that there are many other people who have gone through the same family problems. What they learned can help you, too. The important thing is not to keep your feelings inside.

If you feel hurt that your parents did not consult you when they decided to split up, you may think *not* talking it over with them will make them feel worse. And it just might. But remember that parents need our help and our love just as much as we need theirs. At times like this, they also need to know how we feel, even if it really hurts to tell them.

I also want to talk about kids who always think their parents are going to get a divorce because they see so many bad things happening to people on TV, in movies, and in their own houses. Some parents never fight in front of their kids. Others do. Kids have to remember that even parents who truly love one another sometimes get mad at each other. But that doesn't mean the family will split up.

Mom's House, Dad's House

If your parents do break up, you'll probably end up living most of the time with your mom. But more and more dads are asking to have kids live with them. It's too bad that many moms and dads fight over who will have the kids and when. They want to hurt each other a little more—and they end up hurting the kids. They act like they are in a contest and the winner will get the kids. Sometimes kids want to get back at their parents, too. They go to dad's and complain about mom, and when they get back to mom's house, they complain about dad.

Nobody Likes Divorce

Divorce isn't much fun for anybody. Everybody's angry, sad, and there's lots of yelling and sulking. Worst of all, everybody has to get used to it, whether they like it or not.

That means admitting to people outside the family that things have changed. Sometimes you have to say you live with your mom, other times with dad. It's embarrassing. You might have to miss parties and sleepovers if you have to go to dad's on the weekend, for instance. You might want to go to camp with friends in a neighborhood where you *won't* be for the summer. That's hard.

Divorce can also mean less money for clothes, school supplies, and spending money. You might have to move from a big house to an apartment. If your mom didn't work before, she might need a job now.

You might be home alone after school. When you're staying with dad, he may not be able to entertain you and take you places, because he has money worries. Sometimes he lives in a hotel or tiny apartment that doesn't feel like a home.

When Your Parents Find New People to Love

Most divorced parents eventually want to start a new social life. Most of them end up getting married again. That doesn't happen immediately, but when it does, it's one of the hardest things to welcome a new dad or mom (or both, if both your parents remarry) into your life when you still love the old one.

Parents really want you at least to try to like the new person in their life. You may feel as if you are betraying your real or "natural" mom or dad by being nice to or liking a new one. I have heard that some kids think they can chase away new people by acting up. Sometimes that works, but then your mom or dad will find somebody else. It is hard work to hate people. If they are nice to you and love your mom or dad, this could be a good thing. Sometimes, kids don't like new people who try too hard to be nice. Think of it this way—think how hard it must be to be a stranger trying to make new friends.

There will never be a dad or mom to replace the one you already have, and you should never think so. You can call the new one by his or her first name. If your mom or dad marries again, because you are still a kid you will have to learn that person's rules of the house. She or he may not do things the way you are used to having them done.

There may also be other kids you have to live with. All of you make up what is called a *stepfamily*. In the fairy tale "Cinderella," the stepmother was a miserable woman, and her own daughters were very mean to Cinderella. Because it's such a famous story, kids tend to worry about being a stepchild. They worry that what happened to poor Cinderella will happen to them.

A New Stepfamily

Sometimes the kids who belong to your new stepparent get special treatment from him or her, and you get special treatment from your parent. Somebody is bound to be unhappy. You may feel as if you are not being treated fairly.

On the other hand, a stepparent can also try too hard to make everybody feel loved and wanted in the family—just at the time when you feel down and sad.

You may feel that you hate your new stepparent. That's okay. But hating somebody takes a lot of work. Ask yourself:

1. What do I hate most about that person?
2. What do I like about that person?

It will be so very hard, but try to let those little-bitty "like" feelings come out. Give your stepparent a chance. Give your natural mother or father a chance to be happy, to feel loved and in love again.

If you find the months are dragging on and you still feel angry and down about having a stepparent, it is time to get help. Lots of kids today are in therapy groups where they can talk to grown-ups who know about feelings and with kids their own age. Most schools have social workers or psychologists who can talk to you first and tell you where to go next. Don't put it off, because if you are unhappy, you won't be able to do your best.

When Stepkids Come to Your House

And you thought having brothers and sisters was bad enough! Suddenly you have stepkids on your doorstep (or maybe you are on theirs).

Your natural parent tells you to behave, to treat these new kids nicely and fairly.

But they are not that nice to you. Their natural parent always sides with them in an argument. Your dad or mom sides with you. It's as if you are on different teams. And a family is supposed to be one team.

Here are a few tips to try when you are in this predicament.

1. Make the stepkids feel at home in your home. Share your possessions with them. Do little favors for them. Show them you care.

2. If they're new in your school, introduce them to other kids proudly.

3. Get to know these kids better. Spend time talking to them, showing them you are interested in who they are.

4. Understand that your natural parent and your stepparent are scared. They are unsure of themselves. They want their new relationship to be successful. They want all the kids to get along. Pouting and wishing things were different is only going to make this new family's adjustment harder. Try your best to help make it work.

They're Never Coming Back: How Kids Cope with Death

Girls write me when they are feeling bad. It usually takes a while for me to write back, but I hope that by putting some of their feelings on paper, they begin to feel better already. One of the most miserable times a person can have is when somebody in the family dies. It is hard when a grandparent dies, but if they have lived a long life, it doesn't seem as bad as when a younger person, like a parent, a brother or sister or cousin, or a friend, dies. Not so long ago, grown-ups thought it was better not to tell kids about death. Death was scary and adults felt that if kids were protected from it they would be better off.

When I was doing an episode of "Family Ties" which was about the death of an aunt, the son of one of my own family's best friends was killed in a motorcycle accident. He died on a Wednesday and I had to tape the show on Friday. It was really hard for me to concentrate.

Now kids know more about death, but when death happens to somebody close to you—a mom or dad or brother or sister or cousin or grandparent or friend—it can still be the saddest time in your life.

Kids all say that when this does happen, they think they're the only ones in the world who feel the way they do. That is because not all families are used to talking about the bad and the sad parts of life, so kids can't always get the information they need to make them feel better about what's happened.

Kids say that when they hear this kind of bad news, it feels like a dream—that it isn't really happening to them. They usually have to act very grown-up, just when they feel like acting most like a kid.

Children who lose a parent or somebody else close to them often feel scared about the future. Here are some of their fears:

1. They worry that they are the cause of the death.
2. They think they may die next, or, if their other parent dies, that nobody will want them.
3. They are jealous when brothers or sisters who are also sad manage to get more attention from the family.
4. They feel that their friends don't understand them anymore or don't know what to say to somebody whose parent or brother or sister has died.
5. They worry that the family won't stay together anymore.
6. They worry that they weren't nice enough to the person while he or she was alive.

7. They are angry at the person who died for going away.
8. They are angry when nobody else in the family tells them exactly what happened to the person they loved.
9. They worry about what happens to a person after being buried.

Usually, after a while, the feelings of anger are not as strong anymore. But that doesn't mean kids forget the person who died. Kids have great memories, and when kids love somebody very much, they carry that person's memory with them always. Especially the happy times. But it is very important for a girl to be able to talk about death and to realize that every living thing in the world has its own special lifetime. If there is nobody in your family, at school, church or synagogue, or club you belong to, many city hospitals now have programs for kids like you. You should be able to have your questions answered and to learn as much about death as you need to know to get on with your life again. We all have different ways of feeling better. Some of us like to be with friends. Some of us like to be alone, or with a favorite pet. Some of us write our feelings in a diary or journal, or draw pictures. Some of us want to have reminders of a person who has gone away forever all around us. For some of us that is too painful. Your way of feeling better may not be the same as anybody else's in your family. The important thing is that you feel good about it.

Living through the death of somebody close to you makes you realize how short life is and that we have to live every one of our days to the fullest, by doing our best and being our best.

In a book called *Learning to Say Good-By,* the woman who wrote it, Eda LeShan, says a beautiful thing: "You can never lose a person completely; he or she will be part of you all your life . . . at the same time memories are good to have, life goes on and we need to think about the present and future . . . to do cartwheels again—to express our joy in being alive. That is the very best kind of good-by."

Ask your school or local librarian for this and other books to help you understand what you are going through.

8

My Changing Body

Kids are growing up faster than ever before. At least that's what we keep hearing grown-ups saying. I guess this is because we learn about a lot more things than kids used to.

But it is sometimes hard to be growing up so fast. Sometimes we are just not old enough to understand things that are happening to us. Girls write to me and tell me they are scared about things that are happening to them. They do not always feel that their parents can explain what is happening. Sometimes their parents are too busy. Sometimes their parents are embarrassed to talk about these things. Sometimes we girls don't know how to share our feelings with them. Our parents can't always guess our problems.

It just feels better to have the information we need. I hope this chapter helps you understand your changing body a little bit better.

Keeping Clean

Being clean means a lot to me.

The older we get, the more we need to keep our bodies clean. That is because as we get older, our sweat gets more smelly. It is cute to see a little kid with a dirty face, but it isn't so cute to see a bigger kid with a dirty face.

Here are some tips for keeping squeaky clean:

Where to Wash in the Morning

Every day starts with teeth-brushing and washing up. That includes hands, face, under arms, under nails, neck, and private places.

I usually take a shower in the morning, and sometimes a relaxing bath at night.

Where to Wash at Night

Every day ends with teeth-brushing and washing up in the same places—and your feet, too. Even better, take a shower or a bath. Baths are especially fun with bubbles. Squirt a little shampoo in when you are running the bath water. You should take a bath or shower at least every other day. Especially in the summer when it's hot, a nice cool shower every day really helps you keep fresh.

Washing Hair

Hair should be washed at least three times a week. I wash my hair *every day* because it's the oily

You have to work to have beautiful hair. I wash mine every night.

type. I like newly washed hair. It makes my whole body feel cleaner. If your hair isn't looking as bright as it should, maybe you aren't rinsing the shampoo out well enough. If your hair gets all tangly after washing, use a squirt of conditioner on it, rub it in well, then rinse it out well. Also, keep your hair neat and combed during the day. Hair that is cut or trimmed regularly will be easier to handle and will look better.

Clean Clothes

Clothes should be kept clean. Your underclothes, socks, and tights should be worn only once before being washed. If your parents are too busy to get the clothes washed when you need them, fill up a sink with warm water and a little dish soap or shampoo, and soak your underwear before rinsing them out and hanging them to dry. Keep your school clothes neat by hanging them up or folding them carefully after wearing them. When you drop clothes on the floor, they get all creased and horrible-looking.

Using Deodorant

You will know when to start. It's when you smell something and that something is you. The smell is a little strange. It doesn't smell clean. Under your arms you will feel wet. You will probably have some little hairs growing under your arms at about this time. Guess what? You are really growing up!

I am really surprised by all the girls who don't shower that often and don't ever use deodorant. Maybe you are one of these girls. Maybe you are afraid to try it. Using deodorant is just one more step to growing up and taking care of your changing body. Deodorant keeps you dry under your arms and smelling nice. Ask in your drugstore which deodorant to try. If it doesn't work, try another brand.

Nails

Keep your nails clean. If you don't, you may be carrying germs around under them. I know that some girls love to munch on their nails. Come on, you nail crunchers, get smart. Beautiful-girl nails grow into beautiful-woman nails. There is nothing beautiful about nails that have been eaten away. If you can't stop, ask your family doctor what to do about it.

Using Makeup

I like using a little makeup, and it bugs my mom and dad. They think that girls don't need it. But I am very pale, and I look like a ghost if I don't put just a little color on my face. One of the big questions is, what age can you start wearing makeup?

For most parents, the time when their little girl puts on makeup is very scary—it means she is growing up. So you have to ease into it. Girls who are ten, even eleven don't need it. When you are getting to be twelve and your body is developing, you should talk to your parents about it. They might let you buy some very soft-pink lip gloss and some light blusher to start. If you are younger than this, it's just fun to put on makeup when your friends are sleeping overnight, or you are trying on some of your mom's clothes. Also, if you are like me, your skin might break out if you do not buy *hypoallergenic* makeup. Ask for it in your local store. Put it on carefully in front of a mirror under a good light. You don't want to look like a clown. A little makeup goes a long way. Department stores and beauty-training schools often have free makeup sessions.

Sun Hurts

Makeup can give you pimples, and too much sun can burn your sensitive skin. It is fun to show off a suntan to your friends, but you need your skin for your whole life. Every time you get a burn, you're hurting that skin a little more. The sunburn goes away, but the skin remembers it was burned. It stores up those big, bad rays.

Too much sun makes the skin dry and rough, and wrinkle faster. Wear a t-shirt in the sun, and a hat or sun visor. Wear suntan lotion, too, especially on your shoulders, face, and nose. Be careful in tanning salons. I once went to one and all I got were freckles. Salon tanning can be harsh on the skin, too.

Baby Fat

We can't all be skinny people. Some of us will never be. But eating the right amount of healthy food should get rid of that baby fat. I know some girls who eat too many sweets. Some of them sneak extra food. They act like they don't care if they are fat and slow and can't fit in pretty clothes. But deep down inside they may be very sad. They may just not know what to do. They may not realize that they can change. If you are a girl like this, please ask your school nurse, your family doctor, or somebody you trust to find out how you can lose some of that baby fat. You will be proud you did.

My Body Is Changing Before My Eyes

One day you look like a kid. Then, all of a sudden, you can see your body changing. You are getting not only bigger, you are filling out. You would think that this would be fun for a girl, but it's not. Everybody fights growing up. It is a scary process. It is also exciting.

One of the weird things about growing up is that while we think we want to be more like grown-ups, when it happens to us we want to be small again.

There are some girls who are as young as eight or nine or ten years old when their bodies begin to change. The first change is usually that their breasts get a little bigger. Take it from me, it is a shock! At first, a girl doesn't want to tell anybody about this except her best friend.

Other kids may start teasing her. Her clothes may be suddenly too tight, and what she is trying to hide is easier to see. This is a problem. But it can be solved.

The solution is a training bra. This kind of bra helps a girl keep her growing breasts safe and private. As I said before, it takes a while to get used to, but you will see how much it helps.

Here's a little secret: I hated wearing my first bra. I don't think it was just because it was uncomfortable, or that I didn't want to admit I needed it. I just hated the thought that I would have this piece of cloth around my chest and fastened in the back. It felt funny. It looked funny. But my mom said I needed it. My mom would bug me because sometimes I would

*Can you believe this was me just a few years ago? Girls'
looks change so fast that it's sometimes scary for us.*

try to get away without wearing it! Finally, get this,
she showed me a picture—of me not wearing a bra. I
could see I needed one.

So I began wearing a bra. Bras feel funny at first.

119

But you'd be surprised how soon you forget you have it on. It is also true that a girl's breasts can grow at different rates. One might look bigger than the other. Don't worry. They will eventually even out!

This isn't the end of the change in your body. You will see some hair growing under your arms and in your private place, where it is called pubic hair. All girls have it and it is very natural.

Body Changes:

You will also eventually get your period if you haven't already, probably about a year after your breasts start developing and you have had a two- or three-inch growth spurt. Another word for period is menstruation. A period usually happens about once every month but sometimes not as often as that. It lasts a few days. Some girls get cramps or feel very tired and grumpy. Some don't feel any different than they usually do.

What is a period? This is important to know. It's very weird, and not all moms feel comfortable telling you about things like this. But after all, it's happening to you and it is important, because it means you are a girl who is becoming more like a woman.

One day you may wake up and find blood in your panties. You may be prepared for it, but it is still a shock. Girls get periods when changes in their bodies produce new blood inside the uterus, which is a female body part. When that blood comes out through your vagina, it's your period. At first it might seem like a lot of blood is coming out, but not really. You will get used to it.

You will need to buy some sanitary napkins to wear inside your panties when you have your period. It is easier in the beginning to use napkins than tampons, which you have to learn to insert in your vagina. If you do learn to use tampons, you *must* change them every few hours. The same goes for napkins. Being clean is very important now!

A period is something you will have every month for years and years and years. If you need more information about what to expect, if you don't feel so well when you have your period, if anything at all worries you about what is happening and how it affects your body, ask your mother, the school nurse, your family doctor, or a big sister, if you have one. They will have all the details. Remember that you can do everything you have always done even when you have a period, including swimming (if you wear a tampon). You don't have to rest unless you feel you want to. You should remember to eat healthy food, drink lots of juices and milk, and get enough sleep. Occasionally, girls who eat poorly or are into athletics like long-distance running stop getting their periods. If this happens to you, see a doctor.

Getting your period means you are truly growing up. It means you have a new responsibility to your body.

Don't let anybody tell you that your body isn't important, or that it doesn't matter how you treat it. If you respect your body, other people will, too.

Remember: Girls' bodies change at different times. You should *not* worry if you are the first girl you know to start developing—or the last. Every girl eventually will have what she needs.

Other Kids Do It—Why Shouldn't I?

I'm talking about a few very important things other kids do—smoking and drinking and using drugs—that aren't good for you or me or them.

I am totally against smoking, drinking, and using drugs. Call me square, but I enjoy life and the beauty of it too much to take chances that might hurt me.

Smoking, drinking beer and liquor, and taking drugs can all hurt you, even if you think you're too smart to let them.

Let's take smoking first. Cigarettes are very bad for you. They make your teeth yellow, and they can injure your lungs and your throat. People die from smoking too much for too many years. You want to be your best for your whole, long life—and the time to start is now.

Many adults say they can't stop smoking, or they don't care if it hurts them. I think they are really dumb. Some of you have parents who smoke. You may be worried about them. Ask them to sit down and talk to you about why they smoke. Most parents say they don't want their kids to smoke. They know it is very dangerous. Believe them!

Drinking is just as bad. I'm not talking about apple juice. I'm talking about beer and liquor. There are little kids who drink it. Drinking too much makes your brain sleepy and forgetful and sometimes mean, and the taste is pretty awful. Drinking is not for kids. Life can be a natural high if you let it be.

Drugs are terrible. I hope you go to a school where there are no drugs around. If you do, you are lucky. There are people who sell drugs to kids and don't care what happens to them. What does happen is that these kids get hooked on the drugs. They feel they can't live without them. They stop doing their homework. Some of them steal money from their parents to buy drugs. There are many dangerous kinds of drugs around. If somebody says to you, "Hey, want to try something?" and they show you a pill or a powder that you've never seen before, when they tell you how great you'll feel if you try it, it's up to you to say no. Drugs can make you feel good for a little while. Then they make you feel much worse.

The life we were put on this earth to live is real life. Sometimes real life is hard. Parents break up. Brothers and sisters are mean. Houses burn down. People we love die or go away. Our bodies change and we don't know why. We don't have enough money to buy the things we need. We have to go to sitters while our parents work late hours. We think nobody understands us. Our schoolwork isn't going so well. We have pimples. We don't have good friends. Oh, there are many things to make a kid feel like trying something like drugs.

Drugs and alcohol may make you forget your problems—but not for long. Then you come down to real life and real problems again. I belong to C.A.D.—Children Against Drugs. We travel to schools to tell other kids about the dangers of drugs and to help kids figure out how to make real life work. We tell them that making real life work . . .

- sometimes means asking for help.
- sometimes means making new friends who can help.
- always means having faith in yourself. Having faith in yourself is the key that turns the lock to the mysteries you face as a girl growing up today.

I'm depending on you to be the best you can be. It's the trying that counts, and the harder you try, the happier you will feel about yourself.

Teeth

You've probably got most of your permanent set already. When our twenty baby teeth fall out, thirty-two shiny new ones come in. But they don't stay that way forever if we don't take care of them.

Now don't tell me you're too busy to brush at least twice a day or that you hate the taste of toothpaste. Some brands you can buy today are made especially for kids and taste more like bubblegum than toothpaste. The pumps are fun to use and not more expensive, either.

Oops! There Goes My Only Set of Teeth

When I talk about how important teeth are, I really mean it. When I was seven, I was in the car with my mom. We stopped short and my two front teeth were knocked out. It couldn't have happened at a worse time. I had just gotten the part of Jennifer in "Family Ties." The dentist couldn't save the teeth. Instead, he gave me new ones. Every few years, as my mouth grows, I go in for replacements. It sounds horrible, but I'm used to it. I don't think anybody *likes* going to the dentist, but it's important.

Tina's Toothy Tips to Keep Yours White

Here are my tips for bright, white teeth:

1. Brush every morning after breakfast and again right before you go to bed and be sure to rinse really well. This cuts down on *plaque,* which is the name for all food and bacteria on our teeth that leads to decay.

2. Use floss, that stringy stuff that helps you get places between your teeth that brushing can't reach. This also helps keep your gums healthy. Buy floss coated with wax because it slides between your teeth easier. Ask your dentist how to use it properly the first time.

3. Drink fruit juice every day. Unless your body gets enough vitamin C, your gums can feel sore.

4. Cut down on candy and sweets. It's hard to do, but it's really important. And when you do eat sugary stuff, try to brush soon afterward.

5. Keep your breath smelling fresh. Sometimes, when you eat take-out food or spicy food and don't remember to brush, your breath gets sour. Sometimes this happens when you have cavities that need to be filled. Whatever the reason, bad breath needs to be

stopped. Brushing, flossing, and using mouthwash helps.

6. Even if you do all the right things to your teeth, you still need dental checkups. Sometimes, it takes a long time for a cavity to start hurting. But the smaller it is, the less it will hurt when the dentist puts a filling in it. If you're afraid of going to the dentist, remember that there are many new ways to fix teeth that make it hurt much less than before.

Braces—Who Needs Them???

I've never worn braces, but lots of my friends do. But now I'm getting them! In fact, half of all kids could use braces to straighten their teeth. One out of every five kids needs them badly.

There are many reasons why kids need braces.

1. Because they grew too many teeth and their mouths are crowded and might look a little jumbled up inside.

2. Because they didn't grow enough teeth and there are too many spaces in their mouths.

3. Because when they bite, they can't chew right. This is either because their mouths don't close up all the way when they close them or because they close up too much. Sometimes, their mouths are a little bit crooked.

Sometimes, if you don't get braces to fix up these things, you won't digest your food properly and you may have stomachaches. Sometimes when you can't chew and close your mouth the right way, your jaw will start to hurt.

So that's why lots of kids need braces. And they usually get them starting as early as age six or seven for girls. By the time most girls are about eleven years old, their jaws are finished growing into shape, so dentists like to have the braces on and working by then.

Sometimes, parents don't have the money to spend on braces for their kids. But if you have been told you should have braces, you probably can find a clinic that will help lower the cost of braces. Try to find a clinic that is part of a school for dentists at a university or college near you.

If You're a Metalmouth

Who likes going around with a metalmouth and rubberband smile? I have gotten lots of letters from girls who think they look really ugly with braces. Well, braces never made *anybody* look better. But if you're stuck with them, you can do one of two things:

1. Never smile or open your mouth.
2. Ignore them.

When my friend got braces, she looked different for exactly one day, which was the time it took *me* to get used to the way they looked and for her to get used to having them.

"Don't I look weird?" she asked.

"Very weird," I said. We both laughed. She felt better and so did I. If you're the one getting the braces, remember that it takes much more energy to hide them than it does to flaunt them. Be proud. And if you're the friend of somebody getting braces, try to help her feel better about it. If you're both wired up, start the Secret Society of Metalmouths. That way you can "brace yourself" for anything that happens to you while all those rubberbands and wires and posts are living in your mouths.

And if you have a good friend whose braces are coming out, don't forget to help her celebrate. I'm looking forward to mine!

Seeing the World: When You Need Glasses

Did you know one out of every two people over the age of three wears glasses or contact lenses? For kids, being able to see well is really important, especially to how well we do in school and in our favorite activities. Some of us are farsighted, meaning we can't see things up close; others are nearsighted, which means they can't see things that are far away. Some kids have weak eye muscles that make their eyes wander. My older brother got glasses when he was six. My parents showed him pictures of all the famous people with glasses, including Clark Kent. He took them to school and everybody wanted to wear glasses.

If you find yourself squinting at the bulletin board in your classroom, if the pages of your schoolbooks look blurry, or if your eyes are always tired, then you should see an eye doctor called an ophthalmologist, or an optometrist. If you need glasses, they will send you to an optician, who will fit you with the right frames.

It used to be that girls who wore glasses felt they weren't as pretty as other girls. Now, glasses are sort of like jewelry—if you choose the right ones, they can actually make you look better. Now that contact lenses are popular, girls who wear glasses know that when they get to be teens, they can wear a great "no glasses" look and still be able to see better.

How do I look in glasses? Today glasses are like jewelry and punky hair (like Justine's).

Tina's Tips for "Looking" Good

It is important to remember that we can make our eyes worse by not protecting them. Here are my tips:

1. When you do homework or reading, keep a desk lamp about fifteen inches from your books, at the opposite side of the hand you use to write, with the bottom of the lampshade at eye level. Keep another light in the room on, too.

2. Keep a light on when you are watching television. You can strain your eyes if you sit too close to the TV. Also, you should sit directly in front of the TV, at eye level and not at an angle. If you have to sit closer than ten feet from the TV screen, you should have your eyes checked.

3. When you are having glasses made for you, they should feel just right when they are fitted.

9

My Precious Emotions

If you are like me, sometimes you feel it's great to be who you are.

That usually happens on a beautiful, sunny day when you are having lots of fun.

It also happens when everything is happy in your family life.

It happens when you do your best in school and you can feel proud of yourself.

There are other times when it is not so great to be who you are.

Maybe you have a brother or a sister—or lots of them—and you guys fight all the time.

Maybe your dad and mom don't get along.

Maybe your parents don't live together anymore.

Maybe there isn't enough money for you to buy the clothes and toys you want to have.

Maybe your parents both work and you are alone after school, or have to go to somebody's house to wait for them.

Maybe you aren't doing so great in school.

Maybe you are too shy and nobody talks to you.

Maybe you are too noisy and you can sense that people don't want to be with you.

Maybe you wish you were prettier.

Or thinner.

Or fatter.

Or taller.

Or shorter.

Or that your hair wasn't so curly.

Or so straight.

As you can see, there are many reasons why kids wish and dream that they could be somebody else, or at least very different from who they really are.

I know I am a lucky girl. Everybody tells me that all the time. I get so many letters. Girls say, "I wish I could be you, Tina."

Do you know what? Everybody feels that way sometimes.

Even though I am on a TV show, which is something that other people wish they could do, it's not always that much fun. I have to cram my schoolwork into the day *and* be on a show. Sometimes there's a lot of waiting around the set. It might be a nice day outside, but I am inside the studio or in my dressing room so I can't do sports or anything extra that other kids do. I have to drive to the studio early in the morning, and I sometimes get home when it is dark outside.

So you see, I can get grumpy, too.

What to Do When You Are Grumpy

The problem with the grumps is that while you are having them, you are probably missing out on something great. But you are so busy feeling down that you don't care. Right?

I'm not saying that getting over the grumps is easy. But once you try, you will feel much better.

Tina's Anti-Grump Ideas

1. Good friends can help. That means kids your own age, parents, neighbors, relatives, and teachers. That means anybody you can feel good talking to or helping out.

2. Maybe you have a bad day in school. You go home and your mom is making dinner. Don't just throw your knapsack down and go into your room. Get involved! Help with the shopping or cooking. Share your feelings. I know when I do I feel so much better.

3. Spend time by yourself, away from what makes you grumpy. Don't ask for more of the bad stuff. For instance, if your big brother is a big tease, don't just stand there waiting for him to think up a way to bother you. Listen to music. Draw. Read a book. Shoot baskets. Get your mind clear and calm again.

4. If you feel you can't get over the grumps by yourself, and if nobody in your family can help, look around you. Who is the person you trust the most? That is the person to see right away.

Minor Grumps vs. Major Grumps

There are lots and lots of little things that can make a person who is little (or big) feel bad.

Some of these things are not so important. What I mean is, no matter how bad you feel right now, soon you will feel better. Like if somebody hurts your feelings. A good cry, maybe, and you forget about it.

Some of the things that can make you feel bad are very important, though.

These are your little secrets. You are afraid to tell anybody about them.

Maybe you have been warned *not* to tell anybody.

Maybe you are afraid that, if you do tell, people will laugh at you.

Maybe you have been warned that, if you do tell, nobody will believe you because you are just a kid and kids like to make up things.

Maybe you are afraid that, if you tell, you will get somebody else into trouble.

Maybe you think you are not very important to anybody, that nobody cares about you.

So you keep your secret. A little voice inside you is shouting, "Help me!" But you won't let it out.

Maybe you think about running away.

I know that there are many kids with these feelings and thoughts. I have talked to and made friends with some of them. They are abused children, children who trusted grown-ups or older kids and were forced to see and do things that hurt them, made them angry, and made them sad.

My foster sister, Tina, is one of these kids. I met

her when she lived in a special home-away-from-home
for kids who have told other people their secrets and
are helped to feel better about themselves. Some join
clubs where they can talk about their feelings. They
find they are not as frightened anymore about what has
happened to them.

What does abused mean? It means being hit or
hurt on your body. Sometimes moms get hit. Sometimes it's the kids. Everybody keeps quiet about it.
Everybody is scared.

Being abused also means being touched in your
private areas when you don't want to be touched or
when it hurts.

Maybe you have seen the video called "Strong
Kids, Safe Kids." You can rent it from a video store.
In it, the Fonz from the TV show "Happy Days" tells
kids something that is very, very important:

"Say no."

"Say no" to grown-ups who tell you they want to
be friends with kids and ask kids to be their secret
friends, ask kids to take their clothes off.

If a grown-up or older kid ever asks you to do this
or to play with your private parts under your panties,
then remember what Tina told you:

"Say no."

This person is *not* your special friend. You do not
want a friend who asks you to keep body secrets.

Remember that your body belongs to you. It is so
hard for kids because we trust adults to help us, and
then some of them abuse us instead.

You do not have to share your private parts with

anybody, no matter what they tell you, what they promise you, or who they are. (They might be a neighbor, a parent or stepparent, somebody else in your family, or a teacher or coach.)

I don't mean that your mom can't help you wash properly in the tub. I'm not talking about when your dad or your uncle takes you in his arms and gives you a great big hug. People who love you and respect you want to hug you.

But there are other people who only say they love you when they really are hurting you. You know this deep inside because the hugs feel weird. So

- If you are not very hungry.
- If you can't sleep at night.
- If you have bad dreams.
- If you don't want to go to school.
- If you are afraid of people.
- If you think about running away.
- If you take lots and lots of baths.
- If you blame yourself for what happened,

maybe it is because you were afraid to *"Say no."*

Let me help you feel better about being you. Remember that nobody has the right to hurt you; anybody who does, or who makes you feel really bad, is not a friend. Even if that person is in your own family.

Don't be afraid. Tell somebody what is happening. People who care about children will believe you. If you tell somebody who doesn't believe you, go to somebody else. Be brave. Believe in yourself. Children are protected by laws. You have a right to be protected and safe from anybody who hurts you.

You can ask your librarian for this book about abuse: *No More Secrets* by Oralee Wachter.

You may need to call the following hotline to share a problem: 1-800-4-A-CHILD

You will not be punished for telling. You will feel better. Your family will feel better. Being your best means believing that you are the best. And I know that you are!

10

My Sharing Heart

Whether you live in a small town or large city, there are always people who need your help. You may think you are too young to help anybody much, but that isn't true.

I discovered that kids like us can bring much happiness to other people when I started volunteering at homes for abused children. I would go there once a week with my dad or mom. Of course, the kids were surprised that somebody who appears on TV would bother spending time with them.

But very soon, it didn't seem important that I was on TV. They saw me as a caring person, and that made *me* feel good.

It isn't always pleasant to see people who are suffering. Yet there are families that probably live quite close to you who don't have enough to eat, or a warm place to sleep at night. These people are good people, but they have had bad times and need our help and support.

I give time every week to help people less fortunate than I am. Here I am speaking out for charity.

I am sure that in your area there are many places where you could volunteer to help out.

1. Hospitals always need volunteers. Patients love to hear kids sing. Get a group together for the holidays and sing out. Also, there are many children and older people in hospitals who would love to have somebody read them a book—or just hold their hand. Hospitals usually need magazines and books that are in good condition. Look through your collection and bring some along.

2. Your public library may welcome your offer to stack books, help keep the kids' room quiet during after-school hours, or put up festive art displays. Ask around.

3. At public animal shelters, there is always room for somebody who cares about animals.

4. Senior citizens living in special projects or in nursing homes love to see young faces. They feel cut off from the world and from their own families. You could become a very important part of somebody's life when you volunteer there. If you can't visit on a regular basis, you can make somebody happy by writing them letters. Ask them, in letters back to you, to tell you all about what life was like . . . back when.

5. Mentally and physically handicapped people depend on others to feed them, talk to them, and teach them. Blind people need readers to tell them what's happening in the newspaper. If you are a good reader, check with your community librarian to see if you can record books on tape for the blind to hear.

6. Kids who are angry, who have been abused at home, who have run away, or are trying to recover from using drugs or alcohol, also need new friends, people who won't tell them they have done something wrong and will encourage them to do some things right! Be that kind of person.

7. People in other countries who are less fortunate than we are need our help, too. Old clothes, shoes, canned food, blankets, and other necessities are useful to people after a flood, earthquake, or other tragedy. Get involved through a local organization, or

start one yourself to rid the world of hunger and disease.

8. Adopt your own foreign child. By sending about fifteen dollars a month, you can help a child in another land live a better life. Ask your local minister, priest, or rabbi for some ideas about how you and your friends can sponsor a kid who needs milk, food, clothing, books, and trust. Our family has supported a boy in Africa for five years.

9. Your local park officials may welcome your help cleaning up playgrounds and parks.

10. Collect toys for the Toys for Tots program in your area. This happens at Christmas. Ask your local principal or call your local newspaper to find out when and how to donate toys to this worthy program. Get your class—your whole school—involved! At Halloween, the UNICEF organization raises money to help hungry kids all over the world. Put your bag out front for pennies as well as for candy next time.

Remember: You are never too young to set up business for charity. You could be washing cars, holding a bake sale, getting your old toys and books together for a yard sale right now. There are many things we can do for people. Sometimes we get so wrapped up in our own stuff that we forget about others who are less fortunate.

When I think of all the special things I have been able to do in my life, I realize how important it is to give some of it back. Helping others is one way of saying thanks for what I have. Doing your best to make people smile will make you smile, too.

11

When I Grow Up I Want to Be . . .

T he answer is different for every girl reading this book.

When I grow up I guess I probably will be an actress. But my dad says that maybe I will change my mind.

Sometimes I think I will be a person who helps other people when I grow up.

I like helping other people. It makes me feel good.

Today, girls can grow up and be anything they want to be.

Ask your mother. She will tell you things weren't always like this. Not very long ago, girls didn't think much about what they wanted to be. They had to work extra hard to get the jobs that men didn't want.

Today we girls are very lucky. Why?

1. We know we are as smart and capable as boys.

2. We know we can be whatever we want to be when we grow up.

We can be doctors.
We can be truck drivers.
We can be secretaries.
We can be lawyers.
We can be policemen.
We can be movie directors.
We can be astronauts.
We can be politicians.
We can be firemen.
We can be scientists.
We can be mountain climbers.
We can be newspaper reporters.
We can be pilots.
We can be computer programmers.
We can be anything we want to be.
We can also be moms. We can be moms and workers, too.
We can be the best at anything we try.
That means starting now.

How to Get Ready for the Future

1. *Study hard in school.* Knowing how to read and write and add and subtract and multiply and divide is important. If you are having trouble in school, ask for help—now!

2. *Learn about the world.* Read your local news-

When I grow up I want to be a singer—or an actress or a social worker. Here I am in a recording studio laying down tracks for my first Tri-Tab label album.

paper and magazines, and watch the news on TV. Smart people know what's going on.

3. *Get a head start.* Join clubs, take lessons, read about things you like to do.

4. *Don't worry if you don't know any other girls who like to do what you like to do.* It's okay to be a rocket scientist. You *can* be different—from your friends and other people in your family!

5. *Believe in yourself.* Today you can be a girl and you can be great at whatever you choose to do with your life.

Big Jobs for Small Girls

There are some important jobs you can do right now.

Babysitting

There are a lot of good things about babysitting. You can make money. You can learn how to take care of kids. You can learn to be more responsible (which is what our moms and dads like us to be!). And you can have some fun doing it. I know this because my older sister and brothers used to babysit for me and my brother Cory. And now that I have a little niece and nephew, I can babysit for them myself.

Any job you will take in your life, you have to know something about it before you start. You have to be prepared.

Being a babysitter means taking care of kids. They could be kids in your own family or other people's kids. No matter whose kids they are, they must be treated properly.

Being a babysitter means knowing what to do in all sorts of situations, including emergencies.

Keep these ideas in mind when you take a babysitting job.

1. Get to know the family beforehand. It is a little scary to go to the house of somebody you don't know for the first time.

2. Always ask the parents to write down anything special you should know about the kids—if they are taking medicine, if they have nightmares, how to get in touch with their family doctor, the fire department,

and a neighbor who could help you quickly, and where the parents will be if you need to call them.

3. Kids sometimes try to get babysitters to believe that they should be able to watch TV for hours, eat candy and chips, soda and ice cream, and not have to brush their teeth and wash up before bed. So make sure the parents tell you what the rules of their house are.

4. When you are the boss, don't let kids play near fire, hot water, electrical appliances, heaters, swimming pools, streets, or in busy areas where you may lose them.

5. Don't go babysitting if you are too tired for the job. That's because your job is to stay awake and make sure everything and everybody are fine.

6. Remember that many kids don't really like their parents to leave them with sitters. So you must really work to make them feel you care about them. Read them books. Sing to them. Play games with them. And always clean up afterward!

7. Make sure somebody can drive or walk you home from your job if it is nighttime.

Other Jobs We Can Do *Now*

Yard Work. That includes pulling weeds, trimming hedges, planting gardens, and watering the grass.

Mother's Helper. New moms in your neighborhood and other moms who need help can use you to watch the kids, wash their dishes, and tidy up. In the summertime, some moms will actually take you on a trip with them to help out wherever they go!

Shopper's Assistant. If you know an older person in your neighborhood who can't see the food on the store shelves, or can't carry home heavy bags, you can help them do this.

Errand Person. Kids who live in big cities can help in an office or home by going out and doing important errands in the neighborhood.

Dog Walker. This is a great job if you love animals. You walk people's dogs and keep them company when they are working or on vacation.

Newspaper Carrier. Deliver them in your neighborhood.

When you take a job, it's up to you to do it well. This is called being responsible. If you say to yourself, I'm just a kid, people will understand if I don't do my best, then you will be letting them down—and yourself, too. When you do a job well you feel proud. Being proud is a great feeling. Try it.

Tina's Last—and Best—Words

It is never easy being your best. Being your best means working hard in school. It means learning as much as you can about the world. It means having faith in yourself.

Don't count yourself out.
Dreams are important.

If you have a dream, follow it.

About the Authors

Tina Yothers plays Jennifer on the award-winning NBC comedy "Family Ties." Tina is a veteran of commercials and appeared in the film *Shoot the Moon* with Diane Keaton. Tina is involved in many charities and causes affecting young people and has visited the USSR as a Youth Goodwill Ambassador. She lives with her family near Los Angeles.

Roberta Plutzik is a widely published journalist and author who has written for more than 200 newspapers and magazines here and abroad, including *USA Today, US, The Los Angeles Times, Parade, Glamour, The New York Times, Good Housekeeping,* Canada's *Marquee* and Britain's *She* magazine. Her books include a biography, LIONEL RITCHIE, SUPERSTAR BROTHERS AND SISTERS, THE PRIVATE LIFE OF PARENTS, and BARGAIN CHIC. She is Television Editor at *The Bergen Record Newspaper* in New Jersey, and is married to writer Neil Baldwin. They have two children, Nicholas and Allegra.